THE DAY
OF THE
JACK-O-LANTERN

THE DAY
OF THE
JACK-O-LANTERN

From the Editors
Of *True Story* And
True Confessions

Published by True Renditions, LLC

True Renditions, LLC
105 E. 34th Street, Suite 141
New York, NY 10016

ISBN: 978-1-938877-78-0

Visit us on the web at www.truerenditionsllc.com.

Contents

HALLOWEEN SURPRISE
How My Little Niece Helped Me Find Love.

"Aunt Audrey, you look cute!" Emma-Jean, my five-year-old niece, told me.

I didn't want to disappoint her, but I couldn't believe I was dressed up like a cat—complete with a mask, whiskers, fake fur on my arms, and a long, silver tail. I'm twenty-two, not exactly the right age to go trick-or-treating, but Em had talked me into it.

My older sister, Tracey, had aided and abetted in this, too. Just because she was nine months pregnant, and her husband was out of town on a business trip, she thought she couldn't take her little girl out on Halloween.

Okay, so I could understand why Tracey didn't want to walk around the neighborhood. In fact, when she'd first asked if I'd do it, I was happy to go with Em—my one and only niece. But after agreeing to it, that's when Tracey told me she always dressed up too, and her daughter just loved it. I tried to get out of it, but my sis knew how much I loved my niece and told me how disappointed Em would be if I didn't dress up.

So there we were—Em and me—she, a dog, me a cat—walking the neighborhood streets, knocking on doors of people she knew. I sort of hung back when someone came to the door, although it was a little hard for a grown adult to blend into the shadows with the porch lights on.

A few people looked at me, as if wondering why an adult would be trick or treating—especially when Em would ask for two of whatever they were giving out. "One's for me, and one's for my Aunt Audrey," she'd say. Not that I wanted candy or snacks or little toys.

So every time I got one of those questioning stares from an adult at the door, I reminded myself I was doing this for Em. When kids answered the door, they thought it was pretty neat. They wanted to know who that person was with Emma-Jean, and she'd proudly tell them I was her aunt.

One little boy even called his mom and dad.

"Come and see the big lady! She's a cat. How come you guys don't dress up like that?"

I definitely felt like hiding in the shadows that time—only there weren't any to hide in. And when the boy walked out and handed me my own treat, I couldn't very well tell him I didn't want it. His father sure gave me a funny look, though.

1

We were finally at the last house. After an hour of this, I was ready to go home with Em and shed my cat disguise. Most of the kids seemed to be done for the night, and Tracey had told me to only go in their neighborhood.

Emma-Jean rang the doorbell, and once again, the kids squealed and shrieked when they saw her and then me.

"That is so neat," a little girl about Em's age said. "I wish my folks would dress up like that."

This is the last house, I reminded myself. I can get through this.

"What's your name?" the little boy asked me.

I couldn't very well just ignore them. Four kids were staring at me, waiting for my answer. "I'm Audrey," I finally said.

"Hey, I recognize that voice."

A guy came to the door.

Terry! Oh no, I didn't want him seeing me like this.

I'd dated him in high school. We'd even gone to the Junior Prom, together. For a while, we talked about getting serious, but then, he'd gone to paramedic and firemen's training. I'd gone to college to be a teacher, and we'd lost contact.

I stared at him. He'd been a good-looking kid in high school. Now, he was a very good-looking man. And I had to assume he was still the wonderful guy he'd always been. I had an instant thought of seeing him again, since I'd just broken up with a guy I dated for a year. But it was obvious Terry was married and had kids of his own.

Then I thought, wait a minute. These kids are too old for him. We were both only twenty-two.

"Can you talk?" the little boy asked me. I realized I'd just been standing there, staring at Terry. But of course, no one knew with that cat mask on my face.

"Oh, sorry; yes, I can talk, and yes, I have to admit, I'm Audrey."

"Come off it," Terry said. "It's wonderful to see you, or I guess I should say it's wonderful to hear you, again."

We walked in as I pulled the mask off my face. That sure felt better. Those fake whiskers had been itching the whole evening. I brushed hair out of my eyes; then, I looked at Terry.

"You're just as pretty as ever," he said, softly. He looked at my hand. "No wedding ring or engagement?"

I shook my head. Was he thinking what I was thinking?

"Me, neither," Terry said. "I almost got married, but fortunately, it was called off. She spent all her money on clothes and jewelry, and besides that, I realized I didn't love her enough."

I had to laugh.

"My boyfriend spent his on cars and motorcycles. I told him I'd

2

had enough. That was two months ago, and I've felt total relief ever since I broke it off."

He softly touched my cheek.

"It's good to see you, Audrey. I've missed you. I thought about you over the years, wondered where you were, then heard you were dating someone steady."

"Good to see you too, Terry," I said.

That's when I realized it was awfully quiet in the house. Both Terry and I looked around. There were four little faces staring up at us. Was that a smile on Emma-Jean's face?

And then I wondered, who were the kids, and why was Terry there? So I asked.

He smiled. "These are my nephew and nieces. My sis and her husband had to go visit his mother in the hospital. She fell today and injured herself, maybe a broken hip. I have three days off from the fire station, so I volunteered to come over tonight."

"I hope his mother will be okay. I remember your sister. I liked her a lot," I said. I put my hand on Emma-Jean's head. "And this is my niece. My sis talked me into this, tonight. Just because she's due for a little boy any minute, and her husband is out of town for the night on business, she thought I'd be a good candidate for dressing up like a cat."

"You make a great cat," Terry said.

I felt myself blush. "Oh, we'd better get going. Tracey will be worried about us."

"Call her," Terry said. "Then come in, and we'll talk and the kids can sort through their goodies."

I nodded. When I called Tracey, she thought that was fine. I only told her we were visiting neighbors—not about Terry. I knew she'd tease me about that one, after all the arguments I gave her about dressing up like a cat.

Terry got punch for all of us, and the kids sat at the kitchen table and looked through their prizes for the evening. I told them not to eat any—although I had a feeling they snuck a few pieces of candy in. I could imagine the tummy aches the next day.

My tummy felt a little strange, too. I think it was butterflies, over seeing this guy, again. We talked about the prom and all the fun we'd had together.

"I still have the promise ring I was going to give you," Terry said.

"I didn't know about any promise ring," I said.

It was his turn to blush. "And you didn't know how much you meant to me."

He lightly brushed my cheek with his hand, again. He used to do that a lot when we were in high school, and alone. I liked it, then. I liked it, now.

3

"I have tomorrow night off, too," he whispered. "How about you?"

"I have every night off. I have to grade test papers for my fourth graders tomorrow evening, though."

"How about I come over, and just wait for you while you do that?" he said.

"I think I'd like that. In fact," I said, "I think I'd like that a lot."

He smiled, glanced into the kitchen at the kids who must have been totally absorbed in checking all their treats, then leaned down and softly kissed me on the lips.

It was the same as in high school. Tender and loving and gentle. Only now, it was better. We'd been teens, then. Now, he was a man, and I was a woman.

I knew my folks liked Terry. So did my sister. I'd never hear the end of her teasing me. That was okay. I could be teased, because I knew I'd found, once again, the right man for me.

THE END

This Halloween, Terror Is In!
PHANTOM PROPHECY
A mystifying twist of fate altered my life.

I lay awake, wondering what happened in my life these past few weeks. It was a complete mess.

"Why on earth did you pull out in front of that truck?" I lashed out at my recently dead husband, Charlie.

Charlie always took crazy chances, driving like an idiot, thinking everything would stop for him—even a tractor trailer truck.

The business was going into the ground—now almost defunct, for lack of cash flow.

"Not to worry," I remember Charlie saying with a grin. "We'll be on easy street soon. I've found a virtual gold mine."

I flopped and flounced in the bed. Gold mine—yeah, right. Not only did I miss my scatterbrained mate, I was also furious with him for having such a cavalier attitude toward our livelihood. After I made the payroll this month, I would be flat broke. I was actually thankful that we have no children; I really wouldn't have been able to cope with that.

I finally fell asleep.

Suddenly I woke to thunder and intense lightening.

"Oh, yes," I grumbled. "I really needed this weather." I vaguely remembered the ominous weather report I watched earlier. "All I need is for this weather to damage the house."

I flipped over and tried to drown out Mother Nature with my pillow.

Suddenly, the phone rang.

"My God, who would be calling in this weather, and at this hour?" Probably Mom, making sure I'm all right.

I grabbed the phone and mumbled, "Hello."

No one was there at first—just a hollow sounding line. I almost hung up before I heard a faraway, faint voice. "Nora . . . hey, Nora. . . ." The voice sent icy chills through me.

"Charlie? Oh, no—is this someone playing a nasty joke? This isn't funny!" I slammed the phone down and broke into convulsive, heaving sobs.

I took a deep breath, snatched tissue from the box on my bedside table, and followed the kitchen night light to the fridge. I can't believe someone would do this and in the middle of a storm, too.

Charlie lost his life in the middle of a storm.

"God only knows why you were out that night, Charlie," I said, as I reached for the milk pitcher and leftover pie. When in doubt . . . eat.

I slowly ate a piece of pie and drank the milk, not really tasting anything—just something to keep my hands busy and my mind numb. I put the things away and went back to the bedroom.

Lightning crisscrossed the sky and thunder shook the windows. I hate thunderstorms. Thank goodness the lights didn't go out.

Suddenly, the phone gave another shrill ring.

I froze. Please, not again. I can't take this joking business. But maybe it's Mom this time.

I picked it up and said hello sharply.

"Nora, honey, don't hang up. I can't do too much calling, please."

I almost fainted. "Please, whoever you are, just stop this! It isn't funny!" I started to cry.

"Nora!" the voice said with raw emotion. "I'm sorry, honey, really, I am. Just listen, will you?"

I was too overwrought to even hang up the phone. I saw my white face and large eyes reflected in the dresser mirror.

"Nora, are you listening? I told you we would be all right. Now, listen . . . I have a key in my wallet. I want you to find it and take it to the Wrightsville National Bank tomorrow and get the papers out of the safety deposit box."

The voice sounded so much like Charlie's, but I was still crying.

"Please, Nora, please. I can't call again." The voice faded away and the line went dead.

I banged the phone down. How could anyone be so cruel? I flung myself across the bed and sobbed.

The phone jangled again. I jumped, in spite of myself. It kept ringing, so I finally picked it up.

My mother's voice asked frantically, "Nora, are you all right? You took forever to answer the phone!"

"Nothing, Mom. I—I was asleep." I tried to sound as if I had not been crying.

"Are you sure you're all right? You sound a little funny."

"Fine, Mom. I'm fine." I certainly wasn't going to tell her about the other phone calls.

My mother hung up, telling me to call if I needed her.

I lay across the bed, staring at the ceiling. Wallet? Papers? Key? What on earth did the person on the phone mean? No one knew about the dire straits Charlie and I were in, except Charlie and I. But what if Charlie told someone—an employee—and he was just being vindictive?

What did I do with the stuff the hospital gave me? I got up and went to the desk in the den. I had thrown everything that was in his pockets in the top drawer and had forgotten about it. I reached in the drawer and took out the car keys, wallet, matchbook, and at the bottom, there was loose change. I opened the wallet, went through the few dollars and the cards Charlie kept squirreled away. He kept every card anyone ever gave him.

"Never know when you might need a fellow," he would laugh and say.

Down on one side, where the money was kept, I felt a hard object. "Oh, God, what is this?" I took out a small key with Wrightsville Bank written on it.

I took a deep breath and sat down. How? Why didn't he tell me about this before? And where on earth did that phone call come from?

I did not sleep another minute. I waited until the storm abated some, dressed, and waited some more for daylight and for the bank to open.

I finally drove to the bank, showed my key, and the clerk led me into the vault of boxes. I took out the papers carefully.

They were bonds! They were the missing bonds Charlie always said his Dad had hidden away. He traced them down!

"I thought it was just a pipe dream of Charlie's," I said to the empty vault. I looked them over and knew without a doubt that there was enough for me to get the business back on its feet.

"Charlie, how did you . . . so this was what you were out doing on that stormy evening. You told me you had a surprise for me, but you never made it home. And to think, I may have never looked in that wallet!"

I took the papers, thanked the clerk, and walked to my car. I was still stunned about the bonds, but most of all, about the calls.

I decided to drive to the cemetery and visit Charlie. I drove through the gates toward the back of the cemetery and saw several trucks in the driveway.

A repairman stopped me as I got out of the car. "Sorry, Miss, wires are down around here . . . telephone and electric. Can you come back later?"

I got in my car and he directed me around the circle drive. I looked toward Charlie's grave, wishing with all my heart he were sitting next to me instead.

Then, a sight made me brake so quickly that everything on the seat next to me fell to the floor. My eyes got bigger and bigger, as I stared at my husband's grave. The phone lines were down all right—and laying right across the grave that had Charles Kingston, Rest In Peace chiseled on it.

"My God—that can't be! It just can't!" I grabbed my chest and

7

leaned over the wheel. Now I knew without a doubt that the voice the night before was indeed from beyond. Charlie contacted me the only way he could have.

"Oh, Charlie, was it really you?" Whether it was a coincidence with the phone lines or just fate, Charlie let me know about his surprise, so that my life could go on without worry.

"Thanks, Charlie," I whispered, as I drove out the gates.

THE END

SHE'S OBSESSED WITH HALLOWEEN!
And I can't figure out why

I watched as another car filled with little kids pulled up in front of our house. Smiling jack-o'-lanterns lined our driveway, their flickering candles lighting the way for kids dressed as clowns and ghosts and monsters. It had taken our family two nights to carve all those pumpkins, something we'd done for as long as I could remember.

Mom was sitting, as she had in the past, in front of our garage doors. The double doors were open wide, despite the chilly winds that blew. They were outlined with twinkling orange and white lights to reveal colorful cases full of treats. On each of the cardboard cases that we'd lined up in the garage, my brother and I had painted orange pumpkins and black cats.

This year Mom decided to dress in an angel costume complete with huge, floppy wings. She was a vision in white, even her hair had turned white as snow the past few years. I could see her face as the kids started getting out of the cars. She wore a huge, welcoming smile and her eyes sparkled like a little kid's on Christmas morning.

Mom opened her arms to welcome the first child, a tiny clown. Then came a tall ballerina in a pink tutu, made from what looked like an old slip. There were two ghosts next, just kids with sheets over their heads and holes cut out for their eyes. The last one out of the car had on an old pair of jeans and a sweatshirt with a rubber monster mask over his—or her—head.

And in their hands each of them had an empty pillowcase. The two little ghosts ran to my mother and hugged her. Then they all followed her into the garage. I'd dressed as a cowgirl this year and I, too, welcomed the kids and helped the little ones pick out their treats.

"Can we really have one of everything?" the little clown asked, excitement apparent in her voice.

"You sure can," I said.

And Mom added, "You all just help yourself to some of everything."

The little ones went from one box to the next, barely able to believe they weren't getting just one candy bar. The older ones knew, though. That was plain to see as they led the little ones along the maze of boxes, taking a candy bar from another, then on to the boxes of caramel-coated popcorn, and to a case of juice boxes and one filled with popcorn balls, then to another full of snack bags of peanuts and pretzels.

Last, but hardly least, they got to pick a Halloween toy. Mom and I had shopped and checked catalogs for months finding just the right things. We always got the standard plastic jack-o'-lanterns, then added little fuzzy black cats and bats that bounced from strings. After that, as Mom had done for years, we looked for something to "match" her costume. It was one of those "traditions" that our friends and neighbors had come to expect. This year we'd found tiny angel dolls with gauzy wings.

"Oh, how pretty," the ballerina said as she picked an angel doll for her prize. Throughout the evening I noticed most of the little girls took the angel and the boys as usual took the bats or cats. One boy, though, did pick up an angel and tucked it into a pocket in his jacket.

"Hey, he picked an angel," one of the other boys yelled. "Angels are for girls."

"Angels are for anyone who loves them," my mom quickly said, trying to diffuse the teasing before all the boys got in on it.

The boy that had taken the angel turned on his friend. I thought I detected tears in his eyes behind his monster mask, but his voice was firm. "My mom loves angels. I'm taking it home for her."

I reached out and put an arm around the boy. "Your mom will love the angel," I said. "It's so nice of you to think about her. Why don't you take something for yourself, too?" I could tell he was smiling, even with the mask on, as he reached in and took a bat.

When that small group left we had a little break. There'd been a steady stream of kids for almost an hour. Mom came over and gave me a hug.

"What's that for?" I asked.

"For being such a nice young lady. I saw you talking to that boy and letting him take another toy. That was a kind thing to do, Sandy."

I hugged my mother back. "I learned from the Queen of Kindness," I told her.

She smiled and gave me another hug. Then more kids came up the driveway and it was back to passing out treats and guessing which neighborhood kid might be behind the mask.

Finally—after a couple of hours of non-stop trick-or-treaters— things got very quiet. Our neighbors went in off their porches, some even shut their lights off. But not us. As usual, we waited, knowing there'd be more kids coming down from the projects. It just took them a little longer to get here. But they knew about Mrs. Mullen and her treats. They knew that there'd be enough treats at our house to last them a while.

I don't think it even bothered the kids that most of our neighbors shut their porch lights off just so "those kids from the projects" wouldn't come knocking on their doors. They knew Mrs. Mullen and her family would welcome every one of them.

While we waited, my mind wandered back to when I'd gotten old enough to notice how much money Mom and Dad spent on Halloween treats.

Mom had a jar in the kitchen and she was always putting change in there. If Dad had some overtime, she'd put some bills in, too. When I was really little, I remember asking her what she was saving for because I had a piggy bank where I saved money for the penny candy our corner grocery store sold.

"It's for our Halloween treats, Sandy," she told me with a smile on her face. "You know it takes a lot of money to buy treats for all the kids and to pay for all the pumpkins we carve."

I nodded. I knew how little penny candy I got with my savings so I figured all the candy bars and treats Mom and Dad bought must cost a lot of money.

I had no trouble with that when I was young. It was somewhere after my thirteenth birthday that I started really thinking about the amount of money we spent on Halloween. Mom was always telling my little brother and me that we didn't have money to spend on "foolishness," which was anything we wanted that really wasn't necessary to our health and well-being.

But I loved Halloween and we had such a great time carving all the pumpkins that I never questioned the money spent on buying those pumpkins. And I knew Mom watched for candy sales and bought cases of candy bars or popcorn balls even a couple months before October. She stretched that money in her jar as far as she could stretch it. And for the little toys she gave out, we always made one trip into a large city nearby where there were several wholesale stores. Mom told us how these places sold things to all the bigger stores and they in turn sold them for a higher price.

"That's why they're called wholesale stores," Dad added. "And that's why we come here to get the toys."

"What your dad's trying to say is they're cheap and we can buy three times as many wholesale than we could at the bigger stores back home. Do you understand?"

Myles and I both nodded our heads and Mom smiled, satisfied that we'd learned a lesson in savings. Mom was always big on savings.

As I got older, I didn't much like the stringent rules we had on saving. And it was when I turned fourteen that I began questioning these rules, perhaps testing my parents to see how far I could go.

One day I went too far. I'm sure it was only because I wanted a new pair of jeans for the start of the new school year that I got so hostile about our money situation.

The jeans would've cost almost twenty-five dollars.

Mom looked at that price tag and said, "Sorry, Sandy, this is just too much. We can do better."

"You mean cheaper," I said. "But it won't be these jeans, Mom. Everybody's wearing this kind. I don't want cheap jeans. Just this once, can't we buy good ones?"

"First off, my child, everybody isn't wearing them." Her emphasis was on the every in everybody and I started to shrivel up inside, knowing I was not going to get the jeans I wanted.

"Secondly, cheap jeans don't necessarily mean they're not good ones. It's that little name tag sewn on the back pocket that makes these expensive—expensive, not necessarily good."

"Couldn't we take a little money out of your Halloween jar?" I asked. "It's only August and we could save enough to make it up before October."

"You know I start buying this month, Sandy. That money is set aside for Halloween and we don't use it unless there's a family emergency, and new jeans for you don't constitute an emergency."

Right there in the middle of that department store, I challenged my mother. It was a moment I'll never forget. "You wouldn't have to spend so much on Halloween if you didn't get enough stuff for all the kids from the projects. Most of our neighbors don't even give them anything. Why do we have to? Why do you care so much about them?"

I saw the red creep up Mom's neck and color her cheeks. Her eyes never left mine. It was probably only a couple of seconds till she answered but it felt like an eternity.

"You want to know why I care about those kids from the projects, Sandy?" she asked, but didn't wait for me to answer. "I care about those kids because I see myself and my brothers and sister in each one of them. I lived in the projects and I know how little those kids have." Then she turned and walked out of the store.

I followed a few seconds later, still stunned by her revelation.

My mom had lived in the projects—a place that was built especially for poor people. At least that's what all my friends said. And some of them were poor because they had no dads or their dads were drinkers who spent all the money on booze. At least that's what my friend, Maura, had told me.

All the way home on the bus Mom was quiet and I didn't dare say a word, even though I was dying to know why she had lived in the projects.

When we got home Mom still wasn't speaking to me, though she answered my brother when he asked what was for dinner. Then she got busy in the kitchen. The first time she spoke to me after her

12

startling words back in the department store was to ask me to cut the cucumbers for the salad.

We worked side by side silently until finally Mom sat down at the kitchen table and called me over. "Sit down, Sandy. I think it's time I told you something about my life."

I sat in rapt attention, knowing even at the tender age of fourteen that I was about to hear something that was very important. Something I'd probably remember always.

And I have. Even now, five years later, I can still hear my mother's soft voice as she told me about her life before she met my dad.

"I think you're old enough to hear this story, Sandy. If for no other reason than you questioned why I give so much to the kids from the projects. You must be feeling like I care more about them than about you getting those brand-name jeans."

I started shaking my head. "Mom, I—"

She raised a hand and stopped me. "No, I understand why you're feeling the way you are. That's why I know it's time to tell you about my childhood. And I'm going to tell you so that you'll understand why I care so much about all kids on Halloween, whether they're kids from the neighborhood or kids from the projects."

And so I sat while Mom began to tell me about her own childhood.

"Holidays were never special in our house, Sandy." As Mom said the words, a sadness came over her face, the face I'd only ever seen as content and happy. The only time I'd ever seen Mom sad was when our kitty had to be put to sleep. I felt awful that I'd caused her to be sad.

"At our house," she continued, "holidays were a time for my father to get drunk."

My mind could hardly grasp the fact that my grandfather had been a drunk. All I'd ever known about him was that he'd died before I was born.

"Holidays," she continued, "were a time for us to stay in our bedrooms and hope our father didn't get mad enough to come upstairs and start shouting obscenities at us." She stopped and looked at me. "Do you know what obscenities are, Sandy?"

I nodded, thinking about the words that got one of my classmates in trouble.

I'd definitely heard obscenities. "I know, Mom, but I can't imagine Dad shouting them at me and Myles. That must have been awful for you."

"I'm not telling you this to get your sympathy. I want you to understand, to understand why I care about those kids."

Suddenly, I did understand. I tried to tell her I understood but Mom had drifted back to some other time. I could see that her eyes were looking somewhere way past our kitchen.

"I especially hated it when Daddy swore," she said—although it wasn't like she was talking to me. She was just reliving a bad time in her life and I happened to be there to hear it. "It made me feel awful when he'd say those words that the nuns at our school told us were sinful."

Mom shook her head and sighed. "Holidays were the worst. For whatever reason, our father might be able to go without a drink for five days but come the weekend he was off and running again. And all the big holidays were just like the weekend. They were times to get drunk because he was off work.

"He'd use any excuse to go on a drinking binge," she added.

Mom was getting so agitated it scared me. I reached across the table and patted her hand. "Mom, you don't have to say any more."

She blinked and looked at me. "Oh, sweetie, I'm sorry. I shouldn't have told you all this right now. I wasn't going to until you were older, but when you questioned me at the store, I got angry."

"I know. I shouldn't have done that. I've always known how special Halloween is to you and I had no right to ask you to take money out of that savings for jeans for me. I was just being selfish."

She stood up and put her arms around me. "No, you weren't being selfish. You just wanted something. Teenagers do that sometimes. And maybe in a year or two when your dad gets that promotion, we can get you some really good jeans, okay?"

"Okay."

That had been the end of our talk for the night. After I'd gone to bed I could hear my parents talking, though, and I heard Dad tell my mother that she should tell me everything. I went to sleep wondering what that "everything" was.

The next day, Myles and I went off to school at the same time. But I always got home a half hour earlier because I was in junior high and my brother was still in the grade school.

Mom greeted me at the door and asked me how my day was, but I could tell she had something on her mind. I knew I was going to hear what that "everything" was that Dad mentioned. It both excited and scared me.

"I baked your favorite," she said as I set my books on the hall table. "Come on in the kitchen and have some cookies and milk."

I could smell the chocolate chip cookies when I walked into the kitchen. The aroma and warmth of the kitchen made me feel more comfortable.

"Sit down, Sandy," Mom said. "I'll get us some milk and we can talk." She turned and looked at me. "Your dad thinks you're old enough to hear why I had to go and live in the projects."

I nodded. "If you want to tell me, Mom, I'll listen. And I'm glad you both think I'm old enough to hear about it."

"I'm sure you've been wondering," she said.

Again, I nodded. "It's been on my mind, sure."

"That's why I want to tell you. For one thing, I don't want you to think my whole childhood was awful. Sure my father drank and because he spent so much on drinking we had very little. But my mother made the best of it. Although we rarely had any extra money, Mama still made holidays special for us kids in her own way. Valentine's Day we'd cut hearts out of old newspapers our neighbors threw away and we'd take turns using a red crayon to color them. Mama would hang them up all around the house and it looked so festive. We did the same on St. Paddy's Day, making shamrocks and coloring them green.

"Easter was really special," she went on. "Mama would read us the Easter story. Then," she added with a smile, "we'd color hard-boiled eggs. Mama made dye out of onion skins and beet juice. They were the prettiest colored eggs you ever saw."

"I've heard about dying eggs with natural stuff, Mom," I said. "Our history teacher told us they did that back in the old days."

Mom laughed. I was glad I'd made her laugh, even though I didn't know why.

"Well," she said, "it wasn't exactly the 'old days' when I was a kid. But Mama did know about dying eggs with natural ingredients. And, since we couldn't afford to buy egg dye, the onion skins and beet juice worked just fine."

"Sounds like your mother made holidays really special for you, Mom, even though you didn't have much money."

"She did indeed, Sandy. She did indeed." Mom looked at me with a real soft look in her eyes. "You would've liked your grandma."

"I wish I could have known her."

Mom started getting that sad look again, so I asked her a question to try and get her back to happy thoughts. "But what was it about Halloween that made it so special for you, Mom? Did your mom do something special on that holiday?"

"Well now, Halloween wasn't a holiday that our father had off, yet he managed to spoil that one, too. For me it was worse than the others, even though we still cut pumpkins out of newspaper and colored funny faces on them.

"I think it was seeing all our friends getting so excited as they got ready for trick or treating. They'd start planning their costumes weeks ahead and would talk about what fun it was to go knocking on doors and getting treats. But Daddy didn't allow Mama to buy treats for the neighborhood kids. And, since she was ashamed to be shutting off our porch light on Halloween because she had no treats to give, we weren't allowed to go out and collect any."

I could see this memory made Mom feel bad and was sorry I'd brought it up. I was just about to change the subject again when she did it herself, jumping ahead to memories of Christmastime.

"The big difference in holidays was on Christmas Day. Most of that day was quite pleasant," she said, "because Daddy got drunk on Christmas Eve. All the yelling and swearing was over by morning because he'd finally passed out and stayed in bed most of the day. Mama really pinched pennies to make sure we could have a turkey dinner like all our friends did. And she made our house look cheerful without spending hardly any money."

Mom paused as a smile creased her cheeks. "We all helped string popcorn for the tree that my mother and big sister cut down in the woods behind our house. And Mama would put evergreen branches on the table and mantle and soon the whole house smelled like Christmas.

"It didn't matter that our tree didn't have lights on it and we didn't get presents like our friends, because after our special meal—which we had at noon, while Daddy was still asleep—we sang Christmas songs. Then Mama told us the story of Christmas."

The happy tone in her voice suddenly turned sad again as she said, "I remember hoping I had an angel to watch over me, too, like baby Jesus did. Then, after Mama died, I prayed she'd be my angel in heaven."

I couldn't imagine life without my mother. I could feel Mom's sadness as I thought how awful that must have been for her. "Mom, how old were you when your mother died?"

"I was almost eleven. Too big to cry, yet still little enough to ache from losing my mama's love. It was her that kept us kids going. Me and my big sister and three little brothers—your aunt and uncles— were lost when she died. Daddy expected us kids to keep up the house and cook and clean for him. My sister, your aunt Tyra, was only thirteen, a year younger than you. She couldn't do it all, even though the rest of us tried to help.

"When our father got arrested for hurting a man in a bar one night, the county social workers came. They found out Daddy hadn't been paying any of the bills, so we were pretty much destitute. The woman asked if we had any relatives. The only person we could think of was our father's sister and we'd only seen her a couple of times in our life."

Mom paused, staring off into space and I wondered if she'd ever finish her story.

"Did your aunt take you in?" I asked, trying to bring her back, even as I tried to imagine me and Myles going to live with our aunt.

16

She nodded. "I think she figured she'd get some money, like foster parents do, you know? But we weren't foster kids. We were relatives. So she quit working, telling the social worker she couldn't work and take care of us, too. She went on welfare and became eligible for the low income housing plan that was fairly new back then."

"The projects?" I asked.

She nodded. "They weren't so bad back then. New, like I said. My sister and I had our own bedroom and the boys had theirs. Our aunt wasn't a drunk like her brother, but she wasn't sweet like our mama, either. She yelled a lot and pretty much watched TV all day, letting us kids fend for ourselves. I guess I have to credit her with the good cook I am today. My sister and I either had to cook from what was available or starve. We learned a lot from doing that over the years."

"I should thank her, too, then, Mom. You're the best cook ever."

"Aunt Raquel's gone now, Sandy. She wasn't so bad, I guess. We learned to stay out of her way when her favorite TV shows were on and we made do on what little she gave us.

"Only when we told her there was no food left in the refrigerator did she really lay into us. She'd tell us we shouldn't be crying over not having enough food. That we should be grateful she even took us in or we'd be split up in foster homes and never see each other again.

"That usually kept us quiet even if our bellies were growling. We once went three days eating crackers and water until her next check came."

"Crackers and water?" I asked, unable to imagine eating that for three days.

"Yep. Aunt Raquel spent most of the money she got from the state for us kids on pretty clothes for when she went out with her gentlemen friends. She also had the prettiest robes and slippers for laying around watching TV. So there wasn't a lot of money left for food for five kids."

"Gosh, Mom, that must have been awful."

"Like I said, we managed. The only thing that still hurt a lot was the fact that holidays were no better than before. We didn't have a drunken father on Christmas Eve, but we didn't have our sweet mama, either. There was nowhere around the projects to go cut a tree down and Aunt Raquel wouldn't have let us buy popcorn even if we'd had a tree to string it on.

"The only concession she made for the holiday was letting us have a turkey dinner, which we had to cook, of course. Somehow it didn't seem quite the same, though, without the tree and evergreen smell. At least, not until after dinner when my big sister gathered us all together in her room and told us the Christmas story all over again.

17

It was okay then—even though we cried a little, too, because Mama had been alive the Christmas before."

Tears shimmered in my mom's eyes and I reached out and took her hand in mine. "Oh, Mom, I can't imagine living like that, especially without having a mom. We have so much more than you ever did. I'll never ask for fancy jeans again, I promise."

Mom patted my hand and smiled despite her tears. "Don't you feel bad for the life we have. It's what I swore I'd give my kids." She sighed then and wiped away her tears on her sleeve. "I don't tell many people about this, sweetie. But since you brought up the projects, your dad and I thought you should know."

I nodded, then got up and hugged my mom. "I'm glad you told me. I promise not to be selfish ever again, Mom."

"Sweetie, you're not selfish and you mustn't feel bad when there's something nice that you'd like to have. Like I said, if your dad gets that promotion, we'll be able to get you nicer clothes."

"If Dad gets the promotion maybe we could get more stuff for Halloween."

Mom gave me the biggest smile and hugged me even tighter than before. "I haven't told you yet about why Halloween is so special."

I sat back. Mom was still smiling, so I knew this would be the best part of the story.

"That first Halloween we lived in the projects, my sister timidly asked Aunt Raquel if we could go trick or treating. She said she didn't care. We were so excited because we'd never done it before. We started figuring out how we could make costumes that didn't cost any money. My sister and I took sheets off our beds to make ghost costumes because they were the easiest and we didn't mind the two eye holes we cut in them. Then, for our little brothers we gathered up leaves from the yard outside our building and glued them onto brown paper grocery sacks—with eyes cut out, of course. We even found some branches and stuck them in their shirt sleeves so they really did resemble trees."

I laughed out loud, imagining my uncles dressing up as trees. "Oh, Mom, I can imagine Uncle Rory as a tree, but not Uncle Barry or Uncle Craig."

"Sandy, they were so excited and it was such fun, especially since it was our first time ever to dress up. It didn't matter that we didn't have store-bought costumes. And, just like some of the kids still do, we took a pillowcase off our pillows to gather our treats. The only problem was, people in the projects didn't have much, either, so the treats were few and far between. At some doors we even encountered men like our father who were drunk and shouted at us to get off their property. After a couple of those, we went on home. We wouldn't have dared come down here. We'd been told often enough people down here didn't want to be bothered with us."

Mom stood up and looked out the kitchen window, up toward the hill that led to the projects. It was as though she was back there now, reliving those awful memories.

"Mom, you don't have to say anymore. I understand now. Really I do."

She blinked and turned back toward me. "Oh, sweetie, I'm not sure you can understand. I'm not sure anyone can understand. I remember coming home that night. We each had collected three candy bars, an apple, and a popcorn ball."

Remembering the bags full of treats I'd collected as a kid, I couldn't imagine getting so little.

Suddenly, Mom was smiling again. "You know something, Sandy, when we got home and took those goodies out of our pillowcases, it was like we'd been given a treasure. We savored every bite of those treats. I think the popcorn ball lasted me four days. Although your Uncle Barry ate his treats all at once and got a real tummy ache. He'd never had so many sweets at one time. I guess his system just couldn't handle it."

She was still smiling when she looked me right in the eye and said, "That Halloween was when I made a promise. I promised the good Lord that if I got out of the projects and had a decent life, I would do everything in my power to give children a Halloween they would always remember."

"You sure kept your promise," I said. "Kids at school even talk about our house and how it's the best place ever to go on Halloween."

"I'm glad, sweetie. You know when your dad and I got married, I told him about that promise and he's been good about helping me keep it.

"Before you kids were born, we started off small with just a couple of jack-o'-lanterns and candy bars and apples. Then each year we added a bit more. I started saving and we were able to carve more and more pumpkins and give more treats. When you came along, I started dressing up for the kids and dressed you to match my costume. Word got out about our love of Halloween and that's when the kids from the projects started coming down. Maybe they thought someone who loved Halloween might not mind them coming into town." Mom sighed again, a really deep sigh. I just sat and waited for her to go on.

"Do you know that when some of our neighbors saw them coming, they shut off their porch lights, Sandy. Do you know how that made me feel?"

I shook my head. "It must have made you feel bad."

"It did. It made me feel all the hurt I'd felt as a child. But I tried not to think badly of my neighbors. It just increased my desire to make this holiday special for all children, no matter where they came from. When I remember making do with the treats I got that first Halloween in the projects, I wanted to make sure those kids got enough at my house to last them well into Christmas!"

Mom was smiling again and just in time, because Myles came running in yelling, "I smell chocolate chip cookies." A minute later he was having cookies and milk and telling Mom all about his day.

Watching her as she listened to my kid brother, I couldn't help but think about her and her brothers and sister all those years ago. I didn't think I'd ever look at my mom again without remembering the sad little girl she'd been and the terrible things she'd gone through.

That night I thanked God for my mother and father and my brother. I thanked Him for the food we had and for our home and for us being a family that loved and cared about each other. And I promised Him I'd never forget what my mom told me that day.

"Here they come, Sandy," Mom said, pulling me back to the present. Dad and Myles came out just then, too, knowing we'd need some help with the carloads of kids that were coming down from the projects.

I saw the look of pure joy on Mom's face, and knew I'd always remember where she'd come from. It made her the woman she was today, a woman I loved and admired.

And someday, when I had kids, I knew there'd come a time when I'd tell them the story of their grandmother's life, a woman I'd dubbed the Queen of Kindness.

THE END

LUCKY CHARM
My Cat Found Me A Job And A Date!

I was beginning to think moving to Winter City wasn't such a good idea, after all. As I pulled my mail out of the box that bright October morning, I was greeted with three letters from job interviews: all saying the jobs had been filled. Friends had warned me that small towns could be unfriendly to "outsiders," but I didn't really consider myself an outsider. After all, Grandma Carroll had been a life-long resident—along with many aunts, uncles and cousins who had since moved away. But I always had a fondness for Winter City, mostly because of my growing up years with Grandma Carroll and all of my cousins. So when the real estate office I worked for in Montana closed, I decided to come home.

Winter City was full of happy memories—especially this time of the year. When I was a little girl, and even into my high school years; Grandma Carroll always threw the biggest, best Halloween parties I could remember. All the cousins got together, and had a great time. My folks would drive me down from Wyoming for the event. It was something I looked forward to all year—even more so than Christmas.

The town had changed a lot, since then. Grandma was gone now, and was buried in Riverview Cemetery. The cousins were all grown up and scattered far and wide, raising families of their own. But the little town was still beautiful, with the new art galleries, coffee houses, and quaint little shops. It would never be the same little country town it was when I visited Grandma as a little girl, but I still had a soft spot in my heart for Winter City, and I appreciated the new as well as remembering the old. Still, I was beginning to wonder if I'd done the right thing moving back? But with the expenses of moving, there was no turning back, now. Besides, Ondy, my black cat, was just getting used to her new home.

"I wish I were settling in as well as you, Ondy," I said, patting my purring feline as she lay on the picnic table, soaking up the sun.

That beautiful fall day was just too lovely to waste brooding. I set the job rejections aside, and decided to walk the three blocks to Lonnell's Latte down on the corner. In the short time I'd been back in Winter City, Lonnell's Latte had become my favorite coffee house, and I knew the spiced pumpkin latte would pick up my spirits. The crowd at Lonnell's was always friendly—even though I didn't really know anyone, yet. The patrons seemed to have a smile on their face, and that made me feel good.

Taking a seat on the deck where I could watch the river, I put my worries on the back burner for a while and sipped on the spicy latte—just plain indulging myself.

I was headed home, kicking the fallen leaves from my path when Ondy showed up to meet me.

"Ondy, you're supposed to stay at home!" I scolded.

Keeping a cat confined to the yard was next to impossible, and I knew it. But fortunately, she followed me home obediently.

October advanced, and there was still no promise of work. I was beginning to get nervous and lonely, too. So when I saw the ad for a Halloween costume party at Denton's Tavern, I decided to go. I could sew up a costume in a hurry. Maybe a Raggedy Ann! What I really needed, I decided, was something to get excited about.

It was late afternoon when I realized I hadn't seen Ondy for a while.

"Here, kitty," I called out the back door. Maybe someone's taken her! I panicked. I had heard of people kidnapping black cats around Halloween. Sometimes, they did it for evil reasons!

I hurried to the front door. My heart pounded as I called, "Ondy."

The responding "meow" brought a sigh of relief.

As Ondy marched haughtily through the gate, her tail in the air, I noticed a slip of paper attached to her collar. Unfolding the note, I read:

Your cat has been coming into our place of business. We need to talk. Please call 555-3193.

Just what I needed: another problem! But I dialed the number, prepared for the worst.

"Lonnell's Latte," a male voice answered.

"This is Eunice Garvin," I said. "May I speak to the owner?"

"This is Morgan."

"I'm sorry," I said. "I thought Lonnell was the owner."

"He was the previous owner," Morgan explained. "We just never changed the name."

"I'm sorry," I apologized again, "but my cat came home with a note—"

Morgan laughed, a friendly chuckle that eased my discomfort.

"You mean Latte?"

"Latte?" Her name is Ondy."

"My customers call her Latte," Morgan said. "We all love her; but unfortunately, health department restrictions won't allow her inside, and she's making herself at home on our couch."

"That darn cat," I said. "She's such a people lover. But I really don't know what to do. You can't control a cat like a dog. Maybe she followed me. I come there often for coffee. All I can do is promise if she comes back and you call, I'll come and get her."

"I can relate," Morgan said. "Cats are independent creatures."

He sounded friendly enough, so we left it at that.

The next day, I was busy attaching red yarn to my Raggedy Ann wig when the phone rang.

Please, let it be a job, I thought. But it was Morgan.

"Eunice, Latte—I mean, Ondy—is back," he said, almost apologetically. "Can you come get her?"

Darn cat, I muttered, but I agreed, and set down my project to hurry off to the cafe.

A tall, nice looking young man with sun-streaked brown hair was sitting at a table on the deck, stroking Ondy, who was purring contentedly. Morgan obviously loved cats.

"I'm sorry," I extended my hand. "I'll try to keep her away. I guess I'll just have to quit coming here for coffee."

"I certainly wouldn't want that! "Morgan said, "And you deserve a cup now for making the trip over. This one's on me. What would you like?"

I smiled.

"Spicy Pumpkin Latte is my favorite."

Morgan returned with two steaming mugs.

"So how did you find Winter City?" He asked. "I'm always curious how people get here."

"My grandmother lived here, and I loved visiting here as a kid," I said. "She always had the greatest Halloween parties. My parents would drive all the way down from Wyoming. She made donuts, and we'd have apple cider and—"

"You like Halloween?" Morgan asked.

"Love it," I beamed.

"There's a Halloween party at Denton's Tavern. Would you like to go?"

"I'd love it," I said.

"Actually, I've been making a costume for it. I was planning to go alone. I've been so busy looking for a job, I haven't had time to meet anyone."

"How'd you like to be a barista?" Morgan asked.

"A barista?"

Morgan smiled. "A coffee artist. A barista takes the craft of making lattes, cappuccinos and espressos very seriously. The college kids I had during the summer are gone, and I'm short of help."

"But I don't know a thing about making fancy coffees!"

"I'll teach you."

"But I need a career," I hedged. "I can't just serve coffee for a living."

"All the more reason to give it a try," Morgan said. "Everyone in Winter City hangs out here. If there's a job opening, you'll hear about it."

"And you won't mind if I left?"

"I'll mind," he said, reaching over to pet Ondy's warm fur. "But I won't be upset. I'm used to high turnover."

I smiled as I sipped my latte. "I guess my cat found me a job."

"And a date," Morgan reminded me.

"Yes, to both," I said. "It sounds like fun. And as for our other problem, I'll just try to keep Ondy in the house for a while and break her of the habit of stopping by here."

"I've always heard black cats were bad luck," Morgan said, "but having Ondy come into my shop has been lucky—in more ways than one."

He gathered my sun-warmed Ondy into his arms.

"Mind if I walk you home?" he asked.

THE END

HALLOWEEN HORROR
I Spent The Night In A Cemetery

Wind-whipped gray clouds rolled overhead, looking like something a witch might stir up in her cauldron. Even more ominous were the claps of thunder off in the distance. It was the perfect setting for a special Halloween celebration.

Walking through the spiked iron gates of the cemetery, I was flanked by my husband's best friend, Tate, on one side, while my friend, Susie, brought up the other. Behind us were all the other friends who'd been there for Dennis and me during his long battle with cancer. Most of them were the same people who'd celebrated Halloween with us every year of our nine-year marriage.

"There's Mr. Frankel," I said, spotting the funeral director who'd handled my husband's burial just two months earlier. In the gathering gloom of storm clouds, a backhoe, which was poised near Dennis's grave, looked like a one-armed monster ready to pounce.

The workmen standing by the grave watched our approach with obvious astonishment. They probably hadn't expected people dressed in Halloween costumes to attend the transfer of a body to a different cemetery. But Halloween had been Dennis's favorite holiday, and having made the decision to move his body, it seemed the perfect day.

After being railroaded by my mother-in-law following his death, this was going to be my time to celebrate Dennis's life and to finally mourn his passing.

Mr. Frankel understood my reasons, but I'm sure he hadn't expected so many people at the exhumation. He stepped forward as we approached the site and asked if I was ready to proceed. I had to smile at his valiant attempt to remain composed as men and women dressed in everything from angel costumes to celebrity masks, gathered near the grave.

"It's okay, Mr. Frankel," I said with a smile. "As I told you, Halloween was a special time for us. We met on Halloween, and every year since, our friends have joined us for a costume party. I'm sure Dennis would be pleased that they're all here today to honor his memory."

He glanced around and returned a weak smile. "May we begin then?" he asked. "Those thunderclouds look threatening."

I nodded, and he told the men to proceed.

The backhoe growled into action, its mechanical arm digging deep into the earth above Dennis's casket. Tate and Susie opened the first two bottles of our favorite wine, and we toasted a man whose life had ended much too soon.

Standing amidst our friends, my mind drifted back to the night I met Dennis at a frat house not far from my home. Dennis wasn't in the fraternity, but he and Tate had been invited by some friends. I ended up there because of Susie. She'd practically dragged me out of the house.

"Come on, Rosie," she'd chided me earlier that evening. "Saturday nights are for having fun, not doing laundry."

"Well, old pal," I shot back. "When you're working two jobs all week, Saturday night is the only night to do mundane chores like laundry and cleaning."

"Couldn't your mom help out a little?"

"You know my mom's not up to par, Susie. Her arthritis was bad enough before Dad died. This past year, she's given up trying to fight the pain."

My mother's condition didn't allow her to work, so I'd had to take on a second job after Dad's death, leaving the weekend to do everything else.

"I still think you need a break," Susie went on. "It would do you good to get out and meet new people, maybe even a man."

"Oh, yeah," I said. "Like I'd have time to fit dating into my schedule."

"So ease up on your schedule," she said. "Start taking time for yourself. And start tonight. Just this once, leave the laundry. Take off and enjoy yourself. These frat parties are fun."

Suddenly, fun sounded good. I'd been working non-stop for months. Susie was right, I needed to get out. A Halloween party sounded perfect. I surprised Susie by agreeing to go.

Later, when I told Mom, she surprised me even more. "I'm glad, sweetie," she said. "You work too hard. I've been meaning to tell you to go out and enjoy life." She paused for a second, glancing around her bedroom before continuing. "It would probably help if you didn't have so much upkeep on this place. That's been on my mind a lot. I think it's time to sell. The house is too big for us with your daddy gone."

"But, Mom, I thought—"

She put a finger to my lips, silencing me. "I know what you thought, Rosie. I may be in bed half the time, but I still have a brain that functions. You've taken on all your father's responsibilities, and it's too much. Besides, with my health problems, a two-storey house isn't practical. We're going to sell the house and buy one of those apartments down by the river where everything's on one floor."

"Mom, are you sure you can give up the house?"

"Positive," she said without hesitation. "We've had over a year to heal, and it's time to move on." Her eyes filled with tears as she spoke, and I gave her a hug. "We'll never forget your father, Rosie, but we don't need to live in this house to keep his memory alive. He'll always be in our hearts."

Mom was right, but the thought of selling our home made me sad. It was the only house I'd ever lived in, the only home I'd ever known.

While I got ready to go out, though, reality began to settle in. What a relief it would be not to have the responsibilities that came with the old place. Dad wasn't around to fix a leaking pipe or check out the furnace when it made an awful noise. Repairmen had to be called for those problems, and it cost more than we ever imagined.

By the time Susie picked me up, my heart was lighter than it had been in months. I could actually think about my life again.

Susie was pleased about my news, too. "That'd be great, Rosie. I've missed doing things with you this past year. And even when we did manage a movie or lunch, your mind was always elsewhere—if you weren't falling asleep."

"It's been tough, Susie. Don't ever take your dad for granted. You have no idea the size of the hole in your life when your father is suddenly gone. And I don't mean just to fix things or pay bills or even the awful heartache of holidays without him. It's the everyday stuff that really gets to you. The sadness that engulfs you when you see his chair empty at the dinner table or the sudden awareness that you're never going to see his smile again or feel his arms around you or hear his voice."

"You still miss him a lot, don't you?" she asked.

"Yeah, I do. But enough said. We're going to a party. It's time to put on a smile."

When Susie and I pulled up to a stately old Victorian near the college, the first thing I noticed were the costumed people filling the porch that ran along three sides of the house. Some of the costumes were elaborate, and I wished I'd had more time to put a better one together.

"Wow," Susie said. "Look at those costumes."

"Yeah," I agreed. "Too bad we didn't come up with something more exciting."

"You did better than me," she said, tugging at her old cheerleader's sweater. "I must weigh ten pounds more than I did when I last wore this."

"You look fine," I said, adjusting the red chiffon scarf I'd tied around my forehead. With a puffy sleeved white blouse, an old purple skirt of my mother's, huge gold hoop earrings, and several gold bracelets, I'd hoped to come across as a gypsy. Mom had come to the door as I was leaving with the finishing touch—a small glass bowl turned upside down made a perfect crystal ball.

As Susie took the keys from the ignition, I glanced up at a banner hanging across the railing of the front porch declaring the name of the frat. I didn't notice the rest of the name because at that moment the most handsome man I'd ever seen stepped out the front door.

"What are you looking at?" Susie asked as I stopped and stared. She followed my gaze and smiled. "Oh, I see," she said. "I'd almost forgotten you liked your men tall, dark, and handsome."

"He certainly is," I murmured. By this time, he'd seen me. When his eyes met mine, I couldn't believe the tingly sensation that flooded my entire body. I felt like a silly high school freshman.

"Let's go meet him," Susie said, yanking me out of my stupor.

"I can't."

"What do you mean you can't?" she said.

"I mean I can't move."

She laughed and gave me a little shove. "Just put one foot in front of the other, Gypsy. Remember we came here to party."

I did manage to get to the porch, even as his eyes followed my every step.

When we were only a few feet apart, he smiled. "I've known you forever," he said, breaking the spell his eyes had over me.

"Oh, brother," I said, laughter bubbling up from down deep. "Where'd you get that line?" I hadn't laughed in a long time, and it felt good.

He'd clasped his hand to his chest, rolling his eyes in mock despair while trying not to laugh. "You've wounded me. That wasn't a line."

Then he got serious. When his eyes met mine again, I swore he was looking straight into my soul.

"Where did you come from, angel?" he asked.

"I brought her," Susie interjected, since I was speechless. "And in case you can't tell, she's a gypsy, not an angel."

"Oh, no, she's an angel. I'll thank you for bringing her for the rest of my days," he said, giving Susie a huge smile.

He took my hand, sending a jolt straight through to my heart. "Let's go somewhere quiet," he said. "You can tell me my fortune."

That night was one in a million. It was the closest I'd come to feeling like a princess. Before I left to go home, Dennis and I made plans to meet me the next day.

That Halloween, so many years ago, was the beginning of a joyous love affair I knew would never end.

Despite his death less than ten years later, there was no doubt in my mind that our love would last beyond the grave. I couldn't imagine ever being with another man.

My reverie ended as several of our friends helped the workmen carry Dennis's casket to the waiting hearse. A gust of wind gathered brittle, brown leaves, swirling them around the coffin. I shuddered with the thought of my husband inside, cold and empty of life.

Susie must have seen me tremble and slipped an arm around me as Tate place a wreath of straw flowers on the casket.

"Ride with us to the other cemetery," she said. "We'll swing by later and pick up your truck."

I nodded, allowing her to lead me away from the gaping hole in the earth as I let my mind wander back again to happy times.

After we met, Dennis and I saw each other every day. Our love was instantaneous and all consuming. I could think of nothing else but him. No matter what else I was doing, he was always on my mind.

One evening, as we sat in his car, he kissed me with a tenderness that left me weak in the knees. Passion tore at my insides. "Stop that," my lips whispered, as my body ached for more.

"We can't go on like this, babe," he said. "Let's get married so I don't have to leave you every night."

"Oh, Dennis, yes. I want to be with you always." I sighed, my need for him so strong. Yet I couldn't shake the responsibility I felt for Mom. "But you know I have to get Mom settled in the new apartment first, right?"

He grinned that lopsided grin and said, "Then we better keep the next few weeks free so we can get your mom moved. We'll get married a month after she's in her new place."

I had to return his smile even though I knew it wasn't going to be as easy as it sounded. "Let's give her a couple of months to get settled, okay?"

"Okay, you're worth the wait," he said. "There's no doubt in my mind that we were meant to be together. Nothing will ever change that."

He was right. Our love was the forever-after kind of love my grandma had always told me about. I knew that the night we met.

And everything did work out. We moved Mom in, and she thrived in her new environment. She enjoyed walking along the riverbank during the mornings and evenings, even on snowy days. She still had pain, but a new prescription and her daily walks seemed to give her strength. The move had definitely been a good idea.

Once I was sure she was going to be okay, Dennis and I told her we planned to get married. She was thrilled, hugging us both at the same time. "I'm so happy for you two," she said. "There's something special about your love that I saw from the beginning." Mom's words confirmed my own feelings, and I was thankful she was happy about our decision.

"Dennis," she said. "I'll need your parents' number so I can call and arrange a meeting. Perhaps we can get together for dinner one night so we can get started on the wedding plans."

Dennis hesitated. I knew he wasn't close to his parents, especially his mother. He'd told me their relationship was strained, but he never went into detail, other than the fact that she doted on his younger brother and ignored him. It made me sad, because I'd always felt the love of my parents.

"I'm not sure that would be a good idea," he finally said. "My dad's out of town on business a lot, and my mother, well, let's just say she doesn't care much what I do."

Mom looked distressed. "Dennis, I know she'll want to be a part of your wedding. Why not let me call her?"

Reluctantly, he gave her the number. Two days later, Mom beamed as she told Dennis she'd spoken to his father and made arrangements for his parents and brother to come to dinner the following Sunday.

"I told you it would work out," she said, looking like a cat who'd just eaten a canary.

Dennis was uneasy about the dinner, but he tried not to put a damper on Mom's plans. He even brought a bottle of wine to toast the merging of our families.

Unfortunately, Dennis had been right. His father came alone, telling Mom his wife wasn't feeling well and their son decided to stay home with her. Dennis's mom was a healthy woman. Even if she had been ill, there was no reason for her son to stay with her. Despite it all, we had a good evening with his dad. I was glad Mr. Walters would be a part of our lives, even though I knew my future mother-in-law probably would not.

As our wedding day grew closer, none of us were sure if Mrs. Walters would show up. Even Mr. Walters couldn't guarantee it. "But I'll be there with bells on," he assured us, with a grin so like his son's.

When I walked down the aisle to meet my groom, I was surprised to see Dennis's mother in the front pew. She didn't look happy, but I was pleased she'd come for Dennis's sake.

Later, I found myself wishing she'd stayed home.

She criticized everything, from the small, family ceremony right through to our choice of restaurants for the reception.

"I can't understand why you couldn't have had a bigger wedding," she'd said as we came out of the church I'd belonged to all my life. "Our friends will wonder if you're ashamed of your bride . . . or if she's pregnant."

"Mother," Dennis said through gritted teeth, "Rosie and I wanted to get married quickly, but only because we didn't want the hassle of planning a big affair that takes a year to organize. Besides, her mom isn't wealthy. We didn't want her spending a lot of money. And with me going back to school, we don't have a lot, either."

"I have no idea why you're going back to college, anyway, when you had a perfectly good job at your father's agency," she said.

"I don't want to sell insurance the rest of my life, Mother, but let's save that conversation for another time. This is my wedding day. I'd like to enjoy it."

His mother continued to complain, criticizing the photographer we'd chosen and telling my mother what a poor job the florist had done on the flowers.

Her snide remark as we entered the restaurant for our wedding reception was just about the last straw. "Could you have picked a smaller place?" she asked sarcastically as Dennis's brother grinned behind her, seeming to enjoy our discomfort. I could see my mother wilting under Mrs. Walters's caustic words.

"This was our family's favorite restaurant, Mrs. Walters," I explained. "We felt by having our dinner here, it would be like having a part of my dad here, too."

Dennis's mother actually rolled her eyes. "Well," she said, "we can only hope the food is better than the decor."

"Oh, yes," Dennis's brother, Steve, agreed.

I saw Dennis's jaw working as he gritted his teeth. My own blood was boiling, and I didn't know how much longer I could keep my mouth shut.

At that moment, obviously seeing our distress, Dennis's dad stepped in. He took his wife's arm and quietly said, "Dennis and Rosie, I hope you'll excuse us, but I have to take your mother home. She's apparently not feeling well and needs to leave right now."

His mother began sputtering, "Rob Walters, how dare you—"

But Dennis's dad didn't let her finish. Although he tried lowering his voice, obviously not wanting to cause a scene, his anger had apparently gotten the best of him. "How dare you ruin your son's wedding day?" he countered. "You are a self-centered, selfish woman, and I've about had my fill of your nasty disposition." With that he started to lead her out of the restaurant. Looking back at Dennis's brother, he said, "Are you coming, Steve?"

"Father," Steve said. "It's Dennis's wedding day. Surely someone from our family should be here."

"You're right," Mr. Walters said. "You take your mother home and I'll stay." He handed Steve the car keys and gave him a slight shove toward his mother. "Go. Now."

"But . . . but," Steve stammered, holding the keys. "How will you get home?"

"I'll get a cab. Take your mother home now!"

After Mrs. Walters and her younger son left, my father-in-law turned to us and began to apologize. I stopped him with a kiss on his cheek. "Thank you," I whispered.

Dennis's relief was evident, and finally we were able to enjoy our celebration. My new father-in-law and my mom hit if off well, and my aunt Melanie and her four kids welcomed Dennis graciously into our family. Tate and his wife were equally gracious in assuring me that they had no doubt Dennis had found the perfect woman to be his wife.

Tate even took me aside and told me not to let my new mother-in-law get to me. "She's just a rude, nasty woman," he said. "She always has been. It has nothing to do with you."

Later, Susie, who'd been my maid of honor, told me the same thing. "Don't let her get you down," she said. "Obviously, Dennis's dad knows how to deal with her, and you can take your cue from him. You have a mother, you don't need a mother-in-law who behaves so rudely."

We took everyone's advice. From that day on, we exchanged birthday and Christmas cards with Dennis's mother and called about once a month to keep in touch. I felt we owed her that much. After all, she did give birth to the man I loved. But she was not a part of our lives. Dennis's dad was the only member of his family who visited our home. I came to love my father-in-law deeply and was thankful we had him in our lives.

About a year after our wedding, Dennis's parents divorced.

Eventually, after months of constant harassment, Mr. Walters decided to move out of state to escape his ex-wife's wrath. He stopped by before leaving, and our sadness was apparent.

"Come on, now," Mr. Walters said. "Cheer up. You two can come visit me this summer, and I'll be back for your annual Halloween party and Christmas, too. There's nowhere else I'd rather spend the holidays."

The three of us exchanged a tearful hug, and then Mr. Walters added, "And, of course, if I get lucky and you kids come up with a grandchild for me, I'll be back in a flash."

That made Dennis smile. "Not till I get my degree, Dad," he said. "And that may take a while."

It was tough paying for college and living expenses on my salary, so Dennis insisted on getting a full-time job and finishing his schooling at night. His dad wanted to help, but Mrs. Walters and Steve took most of his earnings.

I hadn't wanted Dennis to work full-time, but he told me there was no hurry in getting his degree. "This way," he said, "we'll be able to save up for a house so we can leave this apartment behind. By the time I get my degree, we'll be settled. I'll start making good money, and we can have lots of babies."

We were both young, so putting off having a family didn't seem all that bad. In fact, after we bought our house, as we sat together on our front porch swing watching the sunset, I was glad we didn't have kids right away. We enjoyed life, reveling in our lovemaking long after our newlywed days.

The only time I ever regretted not having a baby right away was when my dear father-in-law died unexpectedly from a stroke. Dennis's dad had often talked about grandchildren. "When you kids decide to have a baby," he'd told us the last Christmas he'd been with us, "I'm going to spoil the kid rotten. I may even retire just to have extra time to spoil him . . . or her."

I could still recall his smile as he said those words.

Losing Dennis's dad had hurt almost as much as losing my own. We were both hit hard by his sudden death.

It only made matters worse when Steve refused to attend the funeral. "It would hurt Mother," he'd said, angering Dennis.

After the funeral, Dennis seemed to grow more despondent. It wasn't just the sadness that was to be expected, but he seemed tired all the time, too. He could barely finish a day's work, let alone go to his night classes.

I begged him to take a break from his classes, but he told me he was too close to finishing. "Two more semesters, babe, and I'll finally have my degree." I saw the anguish in his eyes as he took me in his arms. "I wish Dad could have been here for that," he said softly.

"I know, honey," I said, wrapping my arms around him. "I wish we could have given him a grandchild, too. But we can't go back. Let's just remember the good times we had with him and hold onto those memories."

He cried then, his tears blending with mine as we held each other close. I hoped our talk had finally broken through his depression.

When Dennis started falling asleep over his dinner, though, and began rubbing his temples as he obviously tried to soothe continual headaches, I knew he was suffering from more than grief; I insisted he go for a checkup.

The doctor gave him some pain pills for the headaches, telling us they could well be from the stress of working full-time, going to night school, and losing his dad on top of it all. But when Dennis got no relief from the pills, his doctor sent him for a brain scan.

The diagnosis was devastating. Dennis had an inoperable brain tumor. It was so large and in such a precarious position, surgery was out of the question. Chemotherapy to stop the tumor's growth was a slim hope, but the only one we had.

A miracle was the only other chance he had, so I prayed for one. We talked to the minister who'd married us, and he agreed that prayer, along with medical treatment, was best. "But try and remember," Pastor Jason told us, "prayers are answered in many ways and in the Lord's good time."

"That's not the kind of answer I want, Pastor," I said. "I want a miracle. I want God to make the tumor disappear."

He smiled at me. "Faith can move mountains, Rosie. Keep on believing, and I'll pray for a miracle for Dennis, too."

For a while, Dennis seemed to respond favorably to the treatments.

"The tumor has definitely stopped growing," the doctor told us after his first course of chemo. "Let's set up another course of treatments in six weeks and see what happens."

I took that as an answer to my prayers. God had stopped the tumor's growth. Maybe next time they'd find the tumor had shrunk. Then it would be gone and we'd have our miracle.

There was no other way for me to think. I refused to even consider the possibility of Dennis's death. He was only thirty-three years old; he was too young to die.

One day, Mom broached the subject with me. She asked me what I would do if the doctors couldn't save Dennis.

"The doctors don't have to, Mom. God can do it. He knows how much I love Dennis. He won't let him die."

Mom looked at me with such obvious distress in her eyes, I had to turn away. "Rosie, sweetheart," she said softly. "Sometimes no matter how much we want something, it just can't be. You have to at least face the possibility that—"

"No, Mom," I cut her off. "No, I don't."

Mom sighed and then changed the subject.

But I couldn't stop Dennis from considering the possibility of death. He insisted we have an attorney draw up a will. "I want to be sure you're provided for, Rosie. Although you'll have the house, truck, and my insurance policy, I want to be certain there's no question that all my belongings go to you."

When I started to protest, he silenced me with a kiss. Then he added playfully, "The way you drive, you could very well go first, and I want to be the sole beneficiary of all your worldly goods, too."

Dennis could make me smile no matter what my mood. "Of course," I said, going along with his attempt to lighten the mood. "I wouldn't want anyone else to get my teddy bear collection or my scrapbooks. Although I'd like Mom to at least have one of the bears, if that's okay with you?"

"I'll let your mom have her choice of the bears." Abruptly, his grin disappeared. "But you have to promise not to let Steve or my mother have anything, Rosie. Promise me."

I shook my head, not wanting to go any further with this discussion.

"Promise me, babe, please," he pleaded. "No one in my family except my dad ever cared about me. I don't want my mother or Steve to have anything."

"All right, I promise."

He nodded. "We'll have it in writing, too, in the will. They won't be able to take anything from you, no matter what they try."

"I don't think they would, honey. Surely, even your mother has some scruples."

"Don't believe it," he said. "Don't trust her, Rosie, not ever. I wish you'd never told them about this cancer," he added. "They've been checking up on me almost every week since you called them."

"Maybe it's because they do care, Dennis. They probably feel bad that you've grown apart. Maybe they're trying to mend fences."

"Have they come here to visit even once?" he asked.

I shook my head. "No, but Steve did bring your mom to the hospital the day you had your first treatment. She even insisted on talking to your doctor. That was a caring thing to do."

"No, babe, you still don't understand. She just wanted all the details so she could get sympathy from her friends. I guarantee you she's milking my illness for all it's worth."

It was hard to believe any mother could be so callous, yet I'd seen the way she'd behaved at our wedding. She'd also cut all ties with Dennis when she learned that we kept in touch with his dad.

Steve and Mrs. Walters insisted Rob had abandoned them, even though Mr. Walters had been generous in the divorce settlement. Mrs. Walters got their house and car, as well as alimony. In addition, Steve's college education was provided for, along with a monthly allowance. Yet Steve didn't even attend his dad's funeral.

Keeping that in mind, I made my promise to Dennis, and we wrote it all in our will. Other than my mother receiving some of my personal belongings, Dennis and I were each other's sole beneficiaries.

Once the will had been drawn up, Dennis seemed to grow stronger. I think he felt everything was in order and he could concentrate on getting his degree. That was his most coveted goal.

Toward the end of that final semester, though, he had to undergo another round of chemo. He struggled valiantly to finish his studies.

He ended up with a 3.9 grade point average. I was so proud of him, I had to do something to celebrate. I planned a party for the night he was to receive his degree, inviting our closest friends and my family to come over after the ceremony. At the last minute, wanting so badly to prove there was some good in Dennis's family, I called and invited them, too.

After speaking to Steve, I was thankful I hadn't mentioned it to Dennis. Steve told me he'd let his mother know but thought she already had plans for that night.

I hesitated, and then I decided to speak my mind. "Steve, you know your brother could die from this cancer."

"You sounded pretty hopeful last time we spoke, Rosie. Is there something you're not telling us?"

"No. The treatments did stop the tumor's growth. But the doctor isn't as hopeful as I am. It would be nice if just once you could be here for him. Your mother's put a wedge between the two of you. Surely you can see that."

"You won't get me to talk against my mother," he said. "Dennis has always been jealous of her love for me. That's why there's a wedge between us, Rosie." He hung up without another word.

I put the conversation out of my mind, and we had a grand time celebrating Dennis's great achievement.

It was definitely one of the best days he'd had in months. Even though the excitement of the party had tired him, for the first time in a long time, we were able to make love. That night our lovemaking was slow and sweet and tender. I felt closer to Dennis than ever.

When we finally lay spent in each other's arms, Dennis said, "Not quite like the good old days, huh, babe?"

"Mmm," I murmured. "Much better. In the good old days, you would have been asleep by now, exhausted from that furious, youthful passion."

He laughed. It was good to hear his laughter. I sighed and snuggled closer against his chest. "I love you, Dennis Walters."

"I love you, Rosie Walters."

Those were the last words Dennis ever spoke. When I woke up, rolling over to kiss him good morning, he was ice cold. I screamed his name, terrified that he'd died in his sleep. Then his eyes fluttered and I put my ear to his chest. I could hear his heart beating. It was faint, but it was beating.

Dialing 911, I offered a quick prayer. Not yet, Lord, please not now, I begged.

At the hospital, Dr. Miller said it was inevitable. My dear, sweet husband had slipped into a coma. He'd struggled for a long time, and his body was worn out. It was as though he'd hung on until he'd achieved his goal.

I sat beside his bed for two days, watching his every breath, continuing to pray, still not ready to let him go.

Dear God, I begged. Please don't take him from me. I don't want to be alone.

During those two days, my family and our friends were there for us. Every day and evening brought more visitors and more prayers. Dennis and I were so blessed to have such support.

When it became apparent that Dennis wasn't coming out of the coma, I asked his doctor if I could take him home. When he was first diagnosed, Dennis had asked me to let him die at home. "I don't want to end my life in a sterile hospital room, babe. Please don't let that happen."

Dr. Miller agreed. He arranged for hospice care, with a nurse coming twice a day to check on Dennis and to prepare me for his death. My mom wanted to be there when I needed a break. But once Dennis came home, I couldn't leave his side. Whatever time Dennis had left would be with me beside him.

Mom tried to get me to go in the other bedroom to sleep, but I refused. Occasionally, I'd drift off for a few minutes, my head leaning on his shoulder. When I'd wake, for just a moment, I'd forget and reach out to pull him close. But there was no answering movement, no loving caress. During those heartwrenching moments, I'd try and focus on that night we'd made love. I thanked God for that last good memory.

On the third morning, I looked at my mother, who'd been solid as a rock for me, apparently at her own expense. I saw the pain etched in her face. "Mom, go home. You need some rest," I told her.

"I'm okay, sweetie."

"You're in pain. I can see it in your face. Go home right now."

"I don't want to leave you," she said.

"Mom, I want you to stay well. I'm going to need you to lean on when—" I couldn't finish.

She agreed then, making me promise to call if I needed anything.

That night, after the visiting nurse left, I turned out the lights and put on a tape Dennis bought me shortly after we met. It was a lovely selection of old love songs. I held Dennis's hand and sang to him. I prayed that even though God hadn't given me a miracle, he might let Dennis hear the music. I also prayed that when death came it would be peaceful. I couldn't bear to think of him gasping for air or going into the spasms that were a possibility with this type of tumor.

The next morning, the fourth day after Dennis came home, he slipped away from me. It was as peaceful a death as anyone could ask for. He sighed deeply, and then his heart's gentle rhythm simply ceased.

He was gone, but I continued to hold his hand, crooning a love song that he would never hear again.

The nurse came in and gently took my hand from his. "It's time to let him go, Rosie."

The finality of her words combined with my exhaustion, and I began to sob uncontrollably. When they came to take Dennis away, I didn't want to let him go.

I vaguely recall the nurse giving me a small, yellow pill. "It'll help," she said. But all it did was cover my pain in a sort of fog. Through the haze that hovered over me, I heard her calling my mother, then I heard her telling me she was going to call Dennis's family.

I tried to stop her, but the words stuck in my throat. I couldn't force them through the fog that had settled over me.

My mother arrived only moments before Dennis's mother and brother. Mom held me, and I felt her tears on my cheek.

When Mrs. Walters walked in, I saw tears in her eyes and wondered why.

Later, as the drug-induced fog lifted, I was able to make out Mom talking to Dennis's mother in the living room. "We should wait until we know what Rosie wants to do," Mom was saying as I shuffled out of our bedroom.

"Do about what?" I asked.

Mom immediately put her arm around me, helping me to a chair.

Mrs. Walters came and stood beside me. "I'm sorry for your loss. I hope you'll let me help you now. I need to do this for my son."

It was hard to believe this was the woman who'd ignored her son for years. Now that it was too late she wanted to help.

"The Walters have a family plot, sweetie. There's a place for Dennis if you want to use it."

"A place?" My mind still wasn't as clear as I'd have liked.

"A grave, sweetheart. A place to bury Dennis."

No, I thought. Dear God, no. I don't want to put him in the ground.

As that horrible thought drifted through my mind, Mrs. Walters went on, telling me she would handle everything. "It will be easier than you going out and looking for a cemetery, Rosie."

Easier, yes it would be easier. I had no desire to look at grave sites.

"It wouldn't do to have Dennis buried anywhere but in the family plot," she added.

When she started talking about their family minister, though, I broke through the silence that had hold of my tongue. "No. Pastor Jason was here for Dennis all through his illness. He knows Dennis. He's been our pastor for the past ten years. Pastor Jason will do the service."

Mrs. Walters sputtered a bit, but my mother intervened. "Rosie's right," she said. "Pastor Jason was at the hospital and here at the house every day. Dennis would have wanted him to officiate."

Finally, Dennis's mother agreed, and she and Mom finished making the arrangements.

I was weary clear through to my bones. Evidently the stress of the past six months had drained me of more energy than I thought. Yet sleep came fitfully as I woke every couple of hours with nightmarish images of caskets and tombstones punctuating my dreams.

Two days later, when everyone had at last paid their last respects and Pastor Jason had spoken eloquently about Dennis's life and our love, I stood with my mother and my best friend on either side of me as the casket was lowered into a yawning hole in the earth. That was the most horrible moment of all.

At the end of that awful day, the day I buried the love of my life, I felt like my own life was over. Mom tried to talk to me, to reassure me that life would go on. "Dennis loved you, Rosie, and he loved life, too. You know he would have wanted you to live life to the fullest."

Of course she was right, but it would be a while before I could even imagine life without him. His side of the bed was so empty. Each morning I'd reach out and grasp nothingness, and the ache in my heart would tear me up again.

Almost a week after the funeral, Mom left to do some shopping. She'd just pulled out of the driveway when the doorbell rang. It was Mrs. Walters and Steve. I hadn't seen or heard from them since the day we'd buried Dennis.

I offered them coffee. They declined. Then Steve suddenly asked if anyone had started Dennis's truck recently. It was such a strange question. Then he explained, "The truck should be run occasionally, Rosie, to keep the battery from going dead."

"Of course," I said, comprehension finally dawning. "I'll try and do that."

"Give me the keys. I'll go out and run the engine for a while."

How odd to have Steve offering to help. Then I remembered him turning down the invitation to see Dennis that last night, and I imagined he must have felt awful about it. I gave him the keys, and then I sat down with Mrs. Walters.

"My friends feel dreadful for me," she said, dabbing at her eyes. "They've all rallied around to try and ease the pain."

I almost reached out to comfort her when I remembered Dennis telling me she'd milk his illness for all it was worth. Apparently, she was using his death to gain more sympathy.

She started asking me questions about how much we owed on the house and about a pocket watch that had once belonged to Dennis's grandfather. "I'd like to keep that in the family, Rosie," she'd said.

I knew what she meant. Dennis's dad had given it to him on our wedding day. It had been his father's, and he wanted Dennis to pass it on to his son.

That thought cut deep into my heart. There'd be no son to pass it

39

on to. Mrs. Walters was probably right. Steve should have it.

Then, as though Dennis were standing right there beside me, I heard his words, "Promise me, babe . . . I don't want them to have anything."

"Uh . . . I'll look for it, Mrs. Walters, when I'm able."

Steve came back in then, and Mrs. Walters immediately rose. "We'll be going now. Call me when you find the watch."

Minutes later, my mother was back, looking a bit flustered. "Rosie, I swear I just saw Dennis's truck down on Division Street."

I shook my head. "It's in the garage, Mom. In fact, Steve went out and—" I stopped, rushing out the back door to find the garage door open and the truck gone. "Steve took it," I said it utter disbelief. "He took the truck." Again, Dennis's words came back to me, "Don't trust her."

After telling Mom what happened, I called Mrs. Walters and demanded that Steve bring the truck back. "You can't just take someone's property, Mrs. Walters."

"Steve would like it as a memento of his brother. I'm sure Dennis would have wanted him to have it."

"No. He didn't want either of you to have anything. In fact, we had a will drawn up a few months ago. We are each other's sole beneficiaries. I'll have my lawyer send you a copy. But right now, I want the truck back in the garage today."

"It's unfair of you to keep everything, Rosie," she shouted.

"It was unfair of you to ignore your son, Mrs. Walters," I shouted back.

"If Steve brings the truck back, will you give him his grandfather's pocket watch?" she asked, as though I hadn't even spoken.

"No. Dennis made me promise not to give either of you anything."

"But . . . but . . ."

"No buts about it," I said, more energized than I'd been in months.

"Then you can't have the truck back," she said.

I felt Dennis's presence once more, and it strengthened my resolve. "Then you'll see your son in jail for theft. If the truck's not back in one hour, I'm calling the police." With that I slammed down the phone.

The truck was returned, but for weeks, Mrs. Walters did her best to try and break the will, demanding that I hand over the pocket watch.

Her efforts failed. And each time she tried, I grew stronger. There was no doubt that Dennis was there with me, helping me through each battle his mother waged. The final one was when she informed me, by registered mail, that I would be denied burial beside my husband. I was not welcome in the family plot.

At that moment, for the first time ever, I felt something akin to hatred in my heart. How could anyone deny a wife a place next to her husband?

That night, on the fringes of sleep, I again felt Dennis's presence and sensed his restlessness. It was almost as though I heard him asking me to let him rest in peace. That feeling led me to do what had to be done.

It took a few weeks to work things out, but with our attorney's help, I was able to get a court order. Then I found the perfect tree-shaded plot in a small cemetery just outside of town, where I would one day be buried beside my husband. All that remained was a call to Mr. Frankel to make the final arrangements.

When he'd asked me which day I'd like to have the casket moved to the new cemetery, I looked at the calendar and saw that Halloween, my husband's favorite holiday, was only two weeks away. It would be the perfect time.

And now here we were, putting my dear husband to rest at last, away from the clutches of a selfish woman who had hardened her heart against her eldest son.

My mother and the rest of our family arrived with our pastor just as the men finished patting down the last of the earth atop Dennis's grave. Pastor Jason read the Twenty-third Psalm, and I felt a sense of peace I'd not known since Dennis's death.

I was confident that he was now at rest, out of his mother's reach. A judge had given me a court order, she could do nothing more.

Tate had brought a smiling jack-o'-lantern to place on the grave. As we walked away in the growing darkness, I glanced back at the flickering candlelight dancing across Dennis's new resting place. In that one moment, I could have sworn the jack-o'-lantern's smile turned into a lopsided grin.

Editor's Note: We received a note from Rosie after she sent us her story. She wanted us to know she had received her miracle, as Pastor Jason had told her, " . . . in the Lord's good time." Rosie is expecting Dennis's baby. God answered her prayer in His own way. She is not alone. And she is certain it is a boy, a son to whom she'll pass on his great-grandfather's gold watch . . . along with loving memories of his father and grandfather.

THE END

HALLOWEEN MISCHIEF
I Was The Pirate's Booty.

It was a struggle getting into my black cat outfit, and I groaned as I looked at my reflection in the bedroom mirror. Turning sideways, I sucked in my tummy, wondering exactly when I'd gained these extra pounds.

It was too late to go out and buy another costume, so it would just have to do, even if I did resemble a kitty that had been lapping up way too much cream!

My five-year-old daughter chose that moment to come charging in. She took one look at me and squealed with laughter. "Mommy's a pussycat!"

My mom chased in after her. "Jamie! Get into your pajamas this minute, young lady."

"Mom, do I look fat in this?" I asked.

She glanced at me. "Of course not, Kelly. You're nice and curvy, the way a woman is supposed to be."

I applied a little make-up, put on a headband with pointed kitty ears attached to it, and picked up my purse. I was going to a party—for the first time in years.

Since Jamie had arrived on the scene my social life had been limited to an occasional trip to the movies with my best friend, Kelsey, which suited me fine to tell the truth. I'd already had my heart broken, married, had a baby, and got a divorce, all in rapid succession. That was enough excitement for one lifetime as far as I was concerned. Now I just wanted a quiet life with Jamie.

The doorbell rang just as I was kissing my daughter good night.

"Have a good time girls!" Mom called out as I left the house with Kelsey.

"This is so exciting!" I giggled as we set off. It was a beautiful night, with a crescent moon suspended like a jewel in the sky, and a pumpkin sitting on nearly every doorstep of our small town. I loved Halloween.

"Jamie had a hard time deciding between being a mermaid or a princess this year," I told Kelsey. "But she's finally decided on being a princess. Keep your fingers crossed she doesn't have another change of heart!" My usually chatty friend was strangely quiet. "Kelsey?" I said.

"Huh?"

"Is everything okay? You're not saying much."

"I'm fine."

"Your costume looks fantastic." She was Princess Leia, her long hair coiled into two buns over her ears.

"Thanks."

Five minutes later we pulled up outside the house that belonged to Kelsey's brother, Brian. I grinned as I reached for the car door.

The house was decorated with cobwebs and spiders, and there were giant plastic rats on the doorstep.

Kelsey suddenly reached out and laid a hand on my arm. "Kelly. Wait."

I turned to her in surprise. "What?"

She bit her lip and looked down. "Trevor is going to be here tonight."

I stared at her, my body going numb. "Please tell me you're kidding."

Kelsey shook her head miserably. "I didn't know how to tell you."

"I knew something was on your mind!" I said. "Well, that's it! I'm going home!"

"And let him know you couldn't deal with seeing him?" she challenged.

"It's not that I can't deal with it . . . I just don't want to see him!" I snapped, feeling panic rise through my body.

"Look, it was all over between you two a long time ago," Kelsey said. "Just say hi and then you can ignore him for the rest of the evening. Come on, we're here to have a good time."

I sighed. If I went home now, would Trevor hear that I'd been too upset to face him?

I didn't want that, so I reluctantly followed Kelsey up the path. The prospect of an evening of fun had abruptly changed. Now I was faced with an ordeal.

As the front door opened, it took every ounce of determination I possessed to step inside. I pasted a big smile on my face because if Trevor saw me I didn't want him to guess how terrified I was. I wanted him to think I never gave him more than a passing thought these days.

I poured myself a cup of punch in the kitchen, my hands trembling.

"Are you okay?" Kelsey asked. "Look, maybe this wasn't such a good idea. You look as white as a ghost."

"I'm fine," I lied.

"I'm going to see if I can find Brian," she said.

I nodded, fighting down another wave of panic as she wandered off.

Trevor had been my high school sweetheart. If I was honest with myself, he was the only guy I'd ever really loved. Looking back, I had no idea why I hadn't been in more of a hurry to settle down. I guess

I'd figured we had forever. It had frustrated Trevor that he couldn't pin me down on a wedding date.

"What's the hurry?" I'd shrugged.

"There is no hurry," he'd replied. "But we've been together for six years now, Kelly, and I'm ready to settle down."

"Well, I'm not," I'd stubbornly insisted. I'd been just twenty-one, and happy with my job at a nearby bank. I loved having some money and a social life and I was a little afraid of swapping all that for the life of a housewife. And I knew I didn't want kids, not right away.

If only I'd talked honestly to Trevor about my feelings. Instead, we'd started arguing, and his anger made me dig in my heels even harder. He'd threatened to leave town, to break off our relationship completely.

"Fine!" I'd yelled. "Go! See if I care!"

Now, years later, regret washed through me. He'd done exactly what he'd said he would—walked out and found a new job in a town thirty miles away.

Several weeks later when he called me, I slammed the phone down in a fury. He never called again, and then a few months later I started hearing rumors. Trevor Adams has a girlfriend. Trevor Adams' girlfriend was pregnant and they were getting married.

The rumors turned out to be true.

The months that followed remain a blur in my memory. There were days I cried non-stop and couldn't get out of bed, followed by days of frantic activity. Mom reminded me that all men were garbage, and I heard again how my dad had walked out when I was just a toddler and how she was really way better off without him.

Eventually, I'd started going out again, but I'd felt like a different woman—one with a stone where her heart used to be.

When Jamie's dad asked me to marry him, I just thought, why not? Nothing seemed to matter anymore, the way it used to. Not surprisingly, my marriage had failed, and Kelsey had told me months ago that Trevor and his wife were divorced now, too. Not that it mattered; it was years too late for Trevor and me.

I took a deep breath. It was time I stopped living in the past. I was here to enjoy myself and that was what I intended to do.

I wandered to the kitchen doorway. Brian had decorated his living room with strings of pumpkin lights that sent a pretty glow over several dancing couples, and to my relief there was no sign of Trevor.

Turning back to the kitchen, I refilled my cup with punch and when I turned around again, there he was.

Seeing him again for the first time in six years felt like being punched in the heart. Trevor was dressed as a pirate, in loose black pants, a white shirt, and a red scarf tied around his head. There was a patch covering one of his eyes and a sword dangled from his waist. He looked devilishly handsome, carefree and dangerous—as if he really did spend his time looting ships for their treasure. My heart pounded as he looked at me.

"It's been a long time, wench," he grinned, speaking in what I guessed was supposed to be a pirate voice.

A small spark of anger ignited deep inside me. This was the man who'd broken my heart and torn my life apart. I hadn't seen him for six years and now here he was, grinning and joking—it was unbelievable!

Suddenly, all I wanted to do was smack the handsome grin right off his face. Instead, I balled my hands into fists at my side and gave him a curt nod. Then I brushed past him into the family room.

Kelsey was dancing, and she shot me an anxious look. Joining her, I forced my body to start moving, too. I wasn't a good dancer at the best of times and I knew I was doing an even worse job than usual—my limbs felt stiff with tension, and my heart was still pounding.

"Are you okay?" Kelsey shouted over the music.

I nodded. "Sure."

From the corner of my eye I saw Trevor swagger into the room. Leaning against the wall, he sipped his drink and watched me intently. I felt my face flush bright red. Why couldn't he just go away?

I was suddenly horribly aware of how pudgy I must've looked in my cat costume, how Trevor must be noticing all the weight I'd gained since he saw me last. But when the music ended he took a step toward me. I fled outside, praying he wouldn't follow.

Pumpkin lights were strung gaily around the trees and bushes in the backyard, and I sank down onto the wooden steps of the deck, wishing I could just disappear into thin air.

My heart filled with dread when I heard footsteps behind me, and I sent a panicky glance over my shoulder, sighing with relief when a couple dressed as Little Red Riding Hood and the Big Bad Wolf came into sight. They disappeared to the far end of the backyard and just as I relaxed again, I heard a voice from behind me.

"Hello, Kelly."

I took a deep breath and let several moments pass before I spoke. "Hello, Trevor."

"Mind if I join you?"

Without waiting for an answer he came and joined me on the steps, handing me a fresh cup of punch. "So how are you?" he asked.

"I'm okay."

"How's your little girl?"

"Jamie's fine."

"I bet you're a fantastic mom."

I made the mistake of turning slightly to look into his face, and only just managed to hold back a gasp. Trevor was gazing straight into my eyes. I opened my mouth to speak, but no words came out.

"I never stopped thinking about you, Kelly," he said softly.

I gazed down into my lap.

"It's the same way with you, isn't it?" he persisted gently.

I shrugged, my heart beating like crazy.

"Kelly?" he prompted gently.

"I don't know!" I snapped, then got quickly to my feet and went indoors.

A couple was leaving and I asked them for a ride, and after a hasty good-bye to Kelsey I left the house.

As cool night air poured into the car I pressed a hand against my heart and took deep breaths, then shut my eyes and tried to think. Trevor was right, of course—I wasn't over him. But that didn't mean I was going to simply tumble back into his arms again after all this time, after the way he'd hurt me. I'd trusted him once, with my whole heart, and look how that had turned out.

"Nice party, hun?' Mom smiled, as I arrived home. "You're home a little earlier than I thought you'd be."

"Trevor was at the party," I whispered.

Mom's eyes widened. "Trevor?"

Tears filled my eyes as I reached up to remove the cat ears attached to my head. "Oh, Mom. . . ."

Her arms went around me and she pulled me close. "I heard he was divorced now," she said bitterly. "I guess he thinks he can come strolling back into your life and just take up where he left off."

"I don't know what to do," I said.

"You don't have to do a thing," she said soothingly.

But I think a part of me sensed a decision would have to be made.

I tossed and turned in bed that night, unable to find any peace of mind. In a way I still loved Trevor and always would. He was my childhood sweetheart, my first love.

Trust, however, was another matter. I'd never be able to trust him again, and it was so unfair of him to talk to me the way he had tonight, to look at me the way he used to.

With a frustrated sigh I flipped onto my back and stared up at the ceiling. Why had Trevor come back into my life? What have I done to deserve this anguish?

My feelings calmed down a little over the next few days and I prayed that Trevor had returned home, even though the thought of never seeing him again brought an ache to my heart.

One morning half way through October, Jamie and I went to the farmers market to hunt for a pumpkin. I loved the traditions of this time of year, the hunting for costumes, the spicy smell of pies baking, carving pumpkins.

Jamie was excited in the car, bouncing around all over the place. When we arrived she tugged me past the stalls selling herbs and winter vegetables to the large field that was an ocean of bright orange, filled with pumpkins of every imaginable shape and size.

Zipping up my jacket against the chilly air, I grinned as I watched Jamie go from pumpkin to pumpkin, marveling at a few that were almost as big as she was.

"Mommy, I want this one. It's gigantic!" she squealed suddenly.

I didn't look up straight away from the medium-sized one I'd just found that would work well for the soup Mom and I made each year. And then I heard Trevor's voice.

"It is gigantic!" he laughed. "You could make a really big, scary Jack O'lantern with that."

I whirled around to find Trevor and Jamie admiring her find. Jamie knew she wasn't allowed to talk to strangers, but was smiling at him shyly.

"Hi, Kelly," he said softly. "This must be your daughter. She's beautiful."

He wasn't in his pirate's costume of course, but he didn't need it to look gorgeous. Even in plain old blue jeans and a brown leather jacket, his black hair ruffled by the breeze, the sight of Trevor was enough to make any normal woman's legs turn to mush.

Inside the pockets of my jacket my fists clenched. I was not going to fall for him again. "Yes, this is Jamie," I said stiffly, then hesitated. "I—I thought you'd left town."

"I'm buying a house here," he smiled.

My heart lurched in shock. "You are?"

He nodded. "I need to be closer to the company I just started work for."

Jamie grunted, and we looked down to find her trying to lift up the giant pumpkin she was determined to take home. Trevor bust out laughing, and in spite of everything, I felt my heart begin to melt. He'd always had a wonderful laugh, uninhibited and infectious, and I was smiling as he helped Jamie lug the pumpkin onto our wagon. I fell into step beside him as he hauled it for us, with Jamie running on ahead.

"My daughter's a little older than Jamie," Trevor told me. "Her name's Millie."

I nodded. "Kelsey told me."

He hesitated. "Millie's smaller than Jamie, though. She was born prematurely. She still has some catching up to do."

I looked at him, wanting to know more, but Jamie chose that

moment to interrupt. She'd found three additional pumpkins and I paid for everything and then began to head back to the car.

"Bye!" I called out to Trevor.

He followed. "How about dinner tonight?"

"No thanks," I said as I put the pumpkins in my car.

"Kelly," he said gently, moving me aside so that he could take over. "Please. I need to talk to you."

I slammed the trunk shut. "What can there possibly be to say?"

"Please," he said again. "I know I hurt you. Let me explain and try to say I'm sorry."

The truth was, I ached to say yes, to spend some time with him. Maybe I was crazy, but I'd been yearning for him for years. I nodded slowly. I'd just hear what he had to say.

"I'll pick you up at seven tonight," Trevor said, and walked away quickly, as if he was afraid I'd change my mind. I climbed into the car, my face flushed, my heart thumping. Have you lost your mind? I asked myself crossly. Have you really just agreed to a date with him?

"I liked that man," Jamie announced from the backseat.

"Did you indeed?" I responded sourly.

"Mommy, he can pick up any pumpkin. He's like superman!" she said.

I nodded weakly, and then tried to change the subject. But as I chatted to Jamie about her costume, my mind was racing. I wished desperately that I had a cell phone number for Trevor so I could call him and say I'd changed my mind. The thought of seeing him tonight filled me with a terrified sort of excitement. Had I made a bad mistake?

Okay, so my life was a bit lonely, but it was a good life. I had Jamie and a decent place to live and the love of my friends and family. I didn't want to give Trevor a chance to hurt me again.

Mom wasn't happy about it. "He broke your heart, Kelly," she said that night, as if I needed reminding.

I fixed on a pair of simple pearl earrings and brushed my dark hair away from my face. "This is just a chance for us to talk," I said.

"About what?" Mom sniffed. "We know what he did to you."

I picked up my purse. "Maybe we both need some closure," I said quietly. "A chance to finally accept what happened and say good-bye to the past."

"Just be careful, okay?" she warned. "Men are all the same— remember that."

"Mom, stop worrying," I said, giving her a quick hug.

When Trevor arrived ten minutes later, Mom stayed in the kitchen banging pots around but Jamie ran to the door in her pink pajamas.

"Hello, Trevor!" she greeted him cheekily.

"Why, good evening, Miss Jamie," he grinned. "I'm here to take your mommy to dinner. Is that okay with you?"

"Oh, yes," Jamie nodded. "I think you should marry her."

I closed my eyes in the embarrassing silence that followed. Jamie was only five, but if only she could keep her thoughts to herself sometimes!

"Good night, honey. Go help Grandma in the kitchen," I said.

I breathed out gratefully as she ran off. Another silence followed as Trevor drove me into town. I glanced once or twice at his profile. It was impossible to tell what he was thinking, although his expression seemed serious.

Memories were tugging at my heart—all the times Trevor and I had driven off somewhere in the battered old Chevy he'd owned as a teen. We'd always been singing along to the radio, or laughing at something silly, not a care in the world. It seemed so strange to be with him again after all this time. So much had changed.

"This is weird, huh?' Trevor said suddenly, as if reading my thoughts. "Being together, going someplace?"

"It sure is," I agreed.

"So what kinds of food do you like these days?" he asked. "I thought we could try out that new place that just opened. Is it any good?"

"I wouldn't know," I said. "I'm a single mom. I don't go to fancy restaurants."

"Right," he said, and then hesitated. "Do you get regular checks from Jamie's dad?"

I laughed bitterly, not sure why I was suddenly acting so snippy. "What do you think?"

Trevor scowled. "Why did you marry that loser in the first place?"

"Because my heart was broken into a thousand pieces and I wasn't thinking straight!" I snapped.

"So it's all my fault?"

"Well, you're the one who walked out!"

"I called you and you hung up on me," Trevor reminded me, his voice tight with frustration.

"Let me out of the car this minute," I said. "I'm going home."

Trevor pulled over and stopped the car, but when I reached for the door he laid a hand gently on my arm. "Kelly."

Something in his voice compelled me to look at him, and when I did the sadness I saw in his eyes made my breath catch in my throat.

"I made a terrible mistake," he said. "I missed you and I was angry and resentful. I wasn't even sure if you still loved me. And then along came Sherra. It all happened so quickly, and I couldn't turn my back when she got pregnant."

"Of course I loved you," I said softly. "I just wasn't ready to get married. I nearly went out of my mind when I heard about you and Sherra." Tears rushed into my eyes.

Trevor hesitated for a moment, then pulled me into his arms. "I'm so sorry."

"Jamie's father was in the right place at the right time," I said. "I was so unhappy and I just needed someone."

It felt so good to be in Trevor's arms again. We'd used to talk like this, cuddled up closely, for hours, sharing our deepest feelings. I looked up at him. "Were you ever happy with Sherra?"

"We both tried," he said. "But I wasn't the man she thought she'd fallen in love with and she wasn't you. We both love Millie, though."

"Of course you do," I said, ignoring the stab of jealousy that pierced my heart at the thought of Trevor having a child with another woman. "Jamie was the only good thing to come out of my marriage."

In an odd way, it was as if we'd never been apart. Trevor and I had always been able to share the most important events of our lives with each other and be completely honest. And by the time he started the car up again and drove the rest of the way to the restaurant, the air between us felt cleared, as if we'd put the past to rest.

Over dinner we chatted and laughed about our children and where life had taken us in the years we'd been apart. I realized that whatever happened I'd always be glad about tonight. The anger and resentfulness I'd nurtured in my heart for so long melted away and I felt nothing but happiness to be with Trevor.

"Can I see you again?" he asked as we walked back to the car.

It was a chilly autumn night but I tingled with warmth. "I'd like that."

Mom was waiting for me when I arrived home and she stared suspiciously at my flushed face. "Oh, Kelly."

"What?" I said, taking off my coat and hanging it up.

"You let him fill your head with a load of sweet talk and promises again, didn't you?" she demanded.

"Of course not," I replied, my blush deepening.

"Men are all the same," Mom reminded me for the thousandth time. "They're no good—not a single one of them."

"Good night, Mom," I said. "Drive home carefully, okay?"

I was grateful to be alone so that I could go over in my mind every second of that night, right up to the moment Trevor had hesitated briefly before brushing a light kiss on my lips.

We'd both wanted a longer, deeper embrace but the way he'd stepped back, the look of restraint on his face told me he was being careful. This time everything between us was going to turn out right.

I hugged myself in bed that night, excited at the thought of tomorrow. I was helping Trevor house hunt! He'd invited Jamie along, too, and he arrived bright and early, just as he'd promised.

"Thanks for doing this," he said. "I'm really going to value your opinion, Kelly."

He glanced into the back seat. "Hey, Jamie, are you going to help me find a nice house?"

She nodded seriously. "It has to have a big yard."

I smiled to myself as Jamie and Trevor began to chat as if they'd known each other all their lives. This felt so right, so good, as if it was meant to be.

We looked at three properties that morning. Trevor dismissed the first two quickly, but we found ourselves lingering in the third. It needed quite a bit of TLC, but the rooms were bright and welcoming and the backyard was huge.

"What do you think?" Trevor asked.

We were standing in the kitchen, which had a large window over the sink overlooking a dormant flowerbed. The sun streamed in. I imagined big dinners being cooked in there, while children ran in and out. I imagined laughter and kisses and long conversations.

"It feels like a home," I said simply.

Trevor nodded. "I like it, too."

And for some reason a tingle of excitement ran through my body.

I asked Kelsey to baby-sit the following night because Trevor had asked me to go out with him again and I couldn't face telling Mom.

My friend turned up fifteen minutes earlier than I'd asked her to bursting with questions and comments.

"Kelly, is this getting serious?" she pressed me, while Jamie spread out craft supplies on the kitchen table.

I bit my lip as a little voice in my head warned me to take things slowly. After all, Trevor had been back in my life for just a matter of days. But Kelsey was my best friend and I couldn't resist telling her what was in my heart.

"I love him," I said. "And even after all this time I believe he feels the same way."

"I knew it!" Kelsey squealed. "I could see it in your face!"

After a delicious meal that night, Trevor and I walked together. It was cold, but neither of us cared as we held hands and talked softly about our lives.

"I can't wait for you to meet Millie," he said. "I think you'll be crazy about her. She's such a sweet, funny kid. I think she and Jamie are going to have a ball."

I squeezed his hand. "I can't wait until you're settled here again. It's going to be wonderful."

He looked at me. "You really liked that house, didn't you?"

51

I nodded slowly, knowing with an absolute certainty that we were going to be together forever. When Trevor took me in his arms I melted against him, passion flickering deep inside, knowing I'd love this man until the day I died.

A few days later Trevor came over to help Jamie and me carve our pumpkins. We had newspapers spread out all over the dining room table as we dug out the seeds and pulpy insides of the pumpkins.

A fire crackled in the fireplace and a pan of spiced cider simmered on the stove. A local radio station was playing a medley of spooky songs. We were all laughing at something when the doorbell rang and the smile on my face faded when I saw Mom. She came inside, and her lips tightened at the sight of Trevor.

"Grandma, it's nearly Halloween!" Jamie said happily, oblivious to the suddenly strained atmosphere. "Trevor is helping me and Mommy make Jack O'lanterns."

"I see that," Mom said. "Hello, Trevor."

"Hello, Mrs. Watkins," Trevor said, getting to his feet.

Mom looked around at the cozy scene, her expression stony. "I guess I haven't come at a good time."

"Oh, don't go Mom. I've made spiced cider," I said quickly.

"I'll come back another time," she said, ignoring me.

"You don't have to go on my account," Trevor said. "I'll leave."

I felt so miserable I could have burst into tears at that moment. Mom's eyes narrowed as she gazed at the man I loved. "I don't want my daughter hurt again."

"Mom, please!" I cried.

"I'll see you and Jamie later," she said, and left the house.

"Sorry about that," I said to Trevor.

"It's okay," he said quietly. "I hurt you and she's not ready to forgive me. It's understandable."

"You hurt Mommy?" Jamie's eyes were huge as she gazed at Trevor.

"A long time ago. And he said he was sorry," I told my daughter.

Jamie immediately relaxed, and gradually the atmosphere did too as we carved faces on our pumpkins.

Mom just needed time, I told myself.

She'd been hurt so badly in the past. My dad had walked out on us when I was a toddler after falling for another woman. After that, Mom insisted she wanted nothing more to do with men. She said they were all the same—uncaring, selfish, and ready to walk over a woman's heart at the drop of a hat.

"Your mom will come around," Trevor said, echoing my thoughts.

Jamie had gone to bed, and our Jack O'lanterns were flickering on the front porch.

"I know," I said, nestling against him.

52

"I'm never going to hurt you again, Kelly. You do know that, don't you?" he asked.

I looked up into his eyes and saw the love I felt reflected back at me. We kissed, and I never wanted to be apart from his again.

With just two days until Halloween. I dropped Jamie at her morning kindergarten session and headed into town. I had an urgent errand. One of the big fake diamonds had fallen out of Jamie's princess crown the night before and I needed to replace it or buy a new one.

Our small main street wasn't particularly busy as I headed for the small novelty shop where I hoped to find what I was looking for. It was cold and I longed for a cup of hot chocolate, deciding to treat myself on the way back. Our town boasted a very nice café that sold gourmet coffees and snacks.

I was lucky and found exactly what Jamie needed to complete her costume—a glitzy pink plastic crown—and I hurried back to the café with it tucked inside my purse. But as I began to push open the café door, I froze. Trevor was seated at one of the tables, with a little girl and a woman I guessed was Sherra.

Millie's mom was so beautiful she could have been a model and the three of them looked like a true family as they smiled and laughed together. Suddenly, I felt freezing cold, inside and out.

Sherra leaned across the table and dabbed at Millie's mouth with a napkin and then she and Trevor got to their feet. Sherra kissed his cheek, and he smiled and slid his arms around her, kissing her back.

I wanted to move, but I was frozen into place, staring in shock at the scene before me. And then Trevor's eyes met mine over Sherra's shoulder, and I spun away, hurrying as fast as I could away from the café. I wanted to run and never stop, to escape my life and all my stupid hopeless dreams.

Instead I went home to cry, the tears already gathering in my eyes as I drove. Fool! Fool! Fool, a voice in my head whispered over and over. I switched on the radio to drown it out, and then changed stations at the sound of a sweet love song.

I didn't want to see Mom, but she was just arriving at the house as I pulled into the driveway. Her eyes widened when she saw my expression, and she followed me inside.

"Kelly, what is it?"

"You were right about Trevor," I said woodenly.

"What do you mean?"

I shook my head, dragging off my jacket and throwing it on the couch. I wanted to die.

"Talk to me," Mom said, but at that moment the doorbell rang.

Wiping at my wet face, I opened it to find Trevor standing there.

He gazed at me anxiously. "For heaven's sake, didn't you see me following you?"

I shook my head. "Just go away."

"Don't you think you're overreacting just a bit?" he demanded. "You saw me with my ex-wife and my daughter. It's Millie's birthday today."

"I saw her kissing you!" I hissed, filled with a terrible jealousy. "And you seemed to thoroughly enjoy yourself!"

He made a helpless gesture with his hands. "What can I say? We try to get along for Millie's sake."

"Yes, I could see that," I snarled.

"We're divorced. You know that," Trevor said, but I didn't want to hear another word.

"Just get out!" I yelled. "I was a fool to trust you again!"

Trevor gave me a long look, his brown eyes filled with sadness. "I thought we'd found each other again, Kelly."

A hard lump entered my throat and in the silence that followed Trevor turned and walked away.

Stunned, I closed the door behind him. It was over. For the second time in my life I'd let Trevor break my heart.

I'd forgotten Mom was in the house. When I turned she was standing watching me and I knew she'd heard every word that had passed between Trevor and me. I waited for her to speak, to tell me I'd done the right thing, but she simply bowed her head.

"You were right about him," I said, tears coursing down my face. "Oh, Mom!"

She took me in her arms. "Oh, Kelly, what have I done?" I thought I heard her say.

Halloween dawned and I'd never felt less like celebrating anything in my life, but I forced a smile as I fixed breakfast for Jamie, trying not to think about the prior day.

Mom had stayed quiet, not saying much even after I explained that I'd seen Trevor with his ex-wife and daughter, all looking so cozy and happy together. She'd fetched Jamie from kindergarten then said she had to leave but would see me later.

It was late afternoon by the time she turned up, but already Jamie was itching to get out and start trick-or-treating.

I'd settled her in front of the TV and there she waited, already dressed in her princess costume, her pumpkin-shaped bucket at her side.

Mom looked into my eyes. "How're you doing?"

"I'm okay," I replied, even though I'd cried myself to sleep the night before and felt as fragile as a kitten. "He's not worth crying over, right?"

54

Mom took two mugs from the cupboard and placed tea bags in them. "He's left town already," she said quietly. "I bumped into Kelsey on the way over here."

"Great!" I said, as my heart twisted painfully. "I hope I never see the rat again as long as I live."

Mom was silent for several moments as she made our tea. "What are you really angry about, Kelly?"

"I told you," I said. "He was with his ex-wife—kissing her!"

"A friendly kiss, am I right? It's good that he's still friends with the mother of his child."

"I can't believe you're defending him," I shook my head incredulously.

Mom bit her lip. "Let's sit down."

I did as I was told, still in a state of disbelief. Was this really my mom who thought all men were rats who could never be trusted? That's what she'd taught me all my life and I just didn't get this.

She sipped her tea, staring thoughtfully into the distance. "A year after your father left he got back in touch with us."

I stared at her. She'd never told me this.

"He wanted me to give him another chance."

Mom's eyes met mine, and I saw the agony and regret buried in her soul.

"I wanted to, Kelly, and I very nearly did. He said he loved us both and begged to be forgiven for his mistake. I loved him, but I just wouldn't let myself forgive and move forward. I was too proud."

"What are you saying?" I whispered. "That I should forgive Trevor?"

"I'm just asking you to think before you let pride ruin your life," Mom said, then added in a voice so soft I had to strain to hear, "the way I let it ruin mine."

I took a long walk that afternoon, while Mom cared for Jamie. I desperately needed to think, to sort through the emotions that were swirling through my brain.

Mom had asked me what I was really angry about and now I repeated the question to myself. Answering honestly was difficult, but I forced myself to do it, as I relived the moment I'd looked through the café window and seen Trevor with his ex-wife and child.

Again, I felt a surge of furious jealousy. Sherra was so beautiful, slimmer than me, and with a rippling curtain of dark, waist-length hair.

I'd wondered how Trevor could possibly love me and not her. And when he'd embraced her, the jealousy had intensified. He had a child with this woman, not to mention years of memories and the fact that they'd always be the parents of such a cute little girl. I'd felt unable to stand it, because Trevor was mine! And, yet, here I was, driving him away.

I sat on a nearby bench and took a deep breath, thinking of the hurt in his eyes when I'd told him to go away. It seemed I hadn't matured much since my teenage years, when I'd stubbornly clung to my anger and refused to repair a rift with the guy I loved the most in the entire world.

Filled with shame, I covered my face with my hands.

If I wanted to be with Trevor I was going to have to grow up because whether I liked it or not he had Millie and an ex-wife. And if I never learned to forgive, I might as well stay single for the rest of my life.

I'd heard that marriage was all about forgiveness, compromise, and acceptance, and for the first time I had an inkling of what those qualities really meant.

Suddenly, I stood and began to hurry back to the house. Maybe it was too late, but I had to let Trevor know how I felt, had to tell him I was sorry.

Kelsey was waiting with my mom at the house as I stumbled inside, breathless from rushing.

"I've got to find Trevor and say I'm sorry!" I gasped. "Mom, could you take Jamie trick-or-treating tonight?"

She nodded. "Don't you worry about Jamie."

Kelsey was scribbling something on a piece of paper. "This is his address, plus directions," she said, pressing it into my hand. "Brian says it's really easy to find."

Mom had rushed off and now returned, thrusting a plastic bag into my hands. I took it, not even bothering to glance inside before I left the house, aware that this was the most important journey I'd ever taken.

I had to show Trevor I wasn't an immature little fool.

The past several days with him had been so wonderful. I'd let him do all the apologizing for the past, but I'd played a part in what went wrong, too. I'd slammed the phone down that day when he'd called.

I shook my head, trying to banish the painful memories. How differently everything might have turned out if I'd only listened to what he had to say. I prayed he'd give me another chance.

It took me two hours to reach the town where he lived and night had fallen as I pulled over to examine the directions Kelsey had given me. I saw that I was just two blocks from the apartment complex Trevor called home, and suddenly I was a nervous wreck.

What if he refused to talk to me? What if I'd lost him for good this time?

I peered into the bag Mom had given me, as if I might discover something that would help. She'd bagged up some sandwiches, a change of clothing, and my cat costume.

Slowly, I drew the soft, black soft fabric from the bag, remembering the night just a few weeks before when Trevor had come back into my life. That had been a special night, and suddenly I couldn't help smiling—one of the most important moments in my life had occurred when I'd been dressed as a cat!

I was alone in the darkness and it took me a few, awkward minutes to wriggle into the costume while seated in my car, then perch the ears on my head.

Trevor had fallen for me all over again seeing me like this. Maybe the magic would repeat itself and he'd be unable to resist me tonight!

I drove the remaining two blocks to his apartment and got out of the car, climbing a flight of steps to his door, which I found ajar. I gave it a light knock and heard his voice from inside.

"Millie, is that you? Did you forget something?"

I licked my lips. "It's . . . it's me," I called out.

There was a silence and then the door was yanked wide open and Trevor stared out at me, his brown eyes widening in astonishment. He was dressed in his pirate costume and looked devastatingly attractive.

"Forgive me?" I asked.

His face dissolved into a smile of such sheer joy that I knew everything was going to be fine. He pulled me into his arms and kissed me, and all the pain and anger in my heart melted away—for good this time.

THE END

GHOSTLY RETURN
Is My House Haunted?

"Ma'am, are you sure you have the right address?" the cab driver asked. "Nobody's lived in that place for a mighty long time."

"Oh, yes, I'm sure. That's where I grew up. I'm going to live there."

"Yes, Ma'am, if you say so," the cabbie said in such a worried tone that it brought back all my doubts and fears in a flash of shivers and goose bumps.

It was twenty years ago that I left this sleepy, southern town, rushing bravely off to the big city to conquer the advertising world with my wit and charm.

For a while, New York let me think I was succeeding. I landed a good job with a well-known agency. I made friends and found a charming little apartment that, while not grand, was all mine. I met an impossibly handsome man who made me think that I was actually all the things I wanted to be. I was making it in the big city! Life was good.

It didn't take but a few years for this perfect life to begin to crumble. I found that the "friends" in the advertising world were fierce competitors whose first priority was getting the best account no matter what they had to do to achieve it. I married the impossibly handsome man and found that he was not nearly as handsome, emotionally or physically, as he seemed. He was at his best only at the beginning of a relationship and he continually looked for new beginnings.

Life ground on for ten years until the competition at work became too ugly and stressful and my husband's unfaithfulness became too painful. There were no children to make us a family, only the constant struggle for more recognition and more things to prove to ourselves how good we were.

I began to long for the peace and quiet of the town that I was in such a hurry to leave. When that longing and the stress finally overcame the satisfaction of the job, the charming apartment, and the handsome husband, I quit the job, divorced the husband, and there I was, back where I started.

The cab driver's doubtful tone of voice, the unbelieving shake of his head, and the worried look in his eyes brought back the flood of doubts and questions I had tried so hard to banish all the way there.

What have I done? The cabbie said no one has lived there for a long time. Why is no one renting it? What happened to the agency that's supposed to take care of it?

The house was willed to me when my mother died. I received all the proper papers along with a key to prove it, but I was too immersed in my city life to care. I couldn't wait to leave my slow-paced lifestyle for the excitement of New York. I didn't want to deal with anything having to do with my hometown, so I turned the property over to the Barnes Real Estate agency to manage, set up a special bank account to receive all rents or revenues and from which to take any taxes or payments due, and ignored the reports and statements that came in the mail.

When we arrived at the once familiar address, I was appalled to see that the three acres of land surrounding it looked like an abandoned wilderness. The house, nearly buried in several summers' worth of kudzu vines and weeds, looked much smaller than I remembered it. That wilderness had once served as playground for me, and a food source for our family. My mother could make anything grow and she always had a magnificent garden that produced a constant supply of fresh vegetables and flowers. We didn't have a lot of money, but we had plenty to eat and fresh flowers to grace our house.

The cab driver stopped the car and looked at me.

"Are you sure you want to stay here, Ma'am? Let me take you to a nice motel. This doesn't look like a place where you should be."

I sighed. It didn't look like that to me, either, but I had burned too many bridges. I had to make this work.

"Will you please wait and let me check it out? I have a key. I'll take a quick look."

"Take your time, Ma'am. I'm not going to leave you here until I know it's all right."

I stepped carefully onto the porch, avoiding the rotting and broken boards. The key I dug out of my purse slid easily into the lock, but didn't unlock the door. Despite the neglect and decay, the front door stood solid and firm and it looked different than the one I remembered.

Reluctantly, I went back to the taxi.

"Will you take me to that motel you mentioned?" I asked. "My key doesn't work and I need to see the rental agency. Somebody changed the locks."

"Yes, Ma'am!" the cabbie said with a smile. "It's probably too late to catch them today, so you'll need a nice place to stay."

He drove me away from my childhood memories quickly, humming a little tune with a smile on his face.

The motel he delivered me to was new and very nice. I was thankful to have someplace to rest from the trip and to rethink my plans. I had no idea my family home had been vacant for so long. Did the agency tell me this and I just didn't pay attention? Or has something happened to the agency and no one notified me of the situation? Barnes Real Estate has been a pillar of the community for as long as I can remember. I can't imagine them letting property they were responsible for fall into ruin and not alerting the owner.

The next morning, after I recovered from a restless and dream-filled night, I ate a quick breakfast in the motel coffee shop and hurried to the town square and the office of Barnes Real Estate.

Except the name on the window was not Barnes's any more. Kirby Realty—Homes and Rentals it said in bold letters.

That explains some of it, I thought, hoping someone at Kirby Realty could explain the rest.

"Good morning," chirped the perky young woman at the desk when I entered. "How can we help you?"

"I'm Rachel Anderson," I said, using my maiden name. "I've come to see about my family's property. The Barneses were managing it and I find it has been abandoned."

"Oh, yes, the old Anderson place," she said. "Let me get Mr. Kirby for you. He knows all about that."

I sank into a straight chair on the other side of her desk and wondered how long Mr. Kirby had known all about my property and why he hadn't contacted me about it. I was beginning to think I had made a big mistake ignoring all those letters.

"Hello, Ms. Anderson. I'm James Kirby. Come into my office and I'll bring you up to date on your property. I gather you didn't receive our letters."

"I probably received them. I just didn't read them," I said. "I haven't been very interested in the property until recently. I thought it was in good hands and everything was taken care of."

"Ah, yes. Well, Mr. Barnes passed away about a year ago and we bought the business. He was well into his eighties and he hadn't kept up with his properties for quite some time."

"I see. The taxi driver told me the place had not been lived in for a while and it certainly hasn't been cared for. The house has practically disappeared in the kudzu vines."

Mr. Kirby cleared his throat. "I'm sorry you had to find it like that. We've been trying to catch up on all the former Barnes properties and we haven't been able to deal with your place yet. According to the records, it was never put up for sale and renters rarely stayed as long as a year. The place is rather isolated and it has a reputation for being haunted."

I shook my head. "Haunted? You must be kidding. A house has to have an unhappy past, a tragedy of some kind, for it to be haunted. There was never a happier place than that house when I was growing up. It can't be haunted."

"I'm afraid that's the reason we get when folks move out soon after they move in. I'm awfully sorry, Ms. Anderson, to be the bearer of bad news."

"What about the bank account for the house? Is there anything left in it?"

"Just a little. The Barneses were careful about taking out only their fee, but there was never much coming in. We haven't taken a fee from it yet, but we haven't done anything with the place yet, either. Now that you're here, we can work on it together."

I sighed. "My key doesn't work. Do you have a new set of keys for it?"

Mr. Kirby rummaged in a box of keys and handed me a set with the name Anderson on the tag. "I believe these are the latest ones. According to the records, several tenants changed the locks. Best if you let somebody know when you go out there. It's probably not a good idea for you to be there by yourself. What are your plans for the place?"

"I plan to live there. Why is it not a good idea for me to be there by myself?" I asked, my tone sharper than I intended as my patience dwindled.

Mr. Kirby sighed. "We think vagrants have been using the house for their own purposes—maybe a kind of halfway house between towns, maybe a headquarters for planning robberies and such. We're not sure, but the records show every time someone moves in, they're treated to noisy and sometimes destructive 'happenings' until they move out. So far, it's been spooky and disturbing, but not deadly. Are you sure you want to live there? We can find you a very nice—and much safer—place closer in to town."

To tell the truth, I was beginning to wonder about that. Do I really want to live there? For a second, I wavered. Then my trained resistance to being derailed from a plan kicked in.

"It's family property. I intend to make it my home again. However, it will take awhile to clean it up, so if you have an inexpensive, small house or apartment I can rent for a month, I could use it. And I'll need some help. Can you recommend someone who is handy at fixing up old houses?"

He looked thoughtful for a few seconds, and then thumbed through a Rolodex file and said, "Yes, I believe I can. His name is Bradley Clark. I understand he grew up around here, left when he graduated high school, and came back a couple of years ago looking worse for his time away, but equipped with a real skill for fixing anything from a leaky roof to a burned-out toaster. He's had plenty of steady work, proved himself dependable, and his fees are very reasonable. I'll call him."

While Mr. Kirby dialed, I wondered if Bradley Clark was a good idea. He sounded like a loser and I didn't need a loser. I was almost ready to tell him to forget it when he hung up.

"You're in luck. Bradley is between jobs and will be glad to help you with the house. He'll meet you there in an hour to see what has to be done. I'll find you a nice place to stay until the house is ready."

"Thank you." I think. Now that things are in motion, I have a creepy feeling that this is a huge mistake, that I should run while I still have the chance.

"Don't worry. Bradley will do a fine job," Mr. Kirby said as if he could read my mind. "He's a little slow on social skills, but he's a genius when it comes to fixing things."

I stopped by the auto rental agency two doors down and rented a car so I wouldn't have to depend on taxi service. When I reached the house, I sat in the car and looked at the depressing scene. It was late September; my favorite time of year, and there was a hint of color in the red oak and maple trees. A frosty morning or two would bring out the glorious golds, oranges, and reds I remember and love.

The job of cleaning up the place enough to live in looked enormous and I was about ready to forget the whole thing and go back to New York when a battered pickup rattled to a stop next to me. A very tall, skinny man unfolded himself from the truck and stood looking at the house.

I got out slowly, my inclination to leave strengthened by this scarecrow of a man.

I took a deep breath and said, "I'm Rachel Anderson and I assume you're Bradley Clark. Do you think this place can be salvaged?"

"Yes, Ma'am."

Whether that meant yes, he's Bradley, or yes, the place can be salvaged, I couldn't tell. He didn't say anything more. He walked around the house, pulling at some of the vegetation as he went. When he finished the circuit, he looked at me.

"Have you got a key?" he asked.

"Oh, yes," I said and fumbled in my purse. I didn't know what to make of him. He was intimidating and fascinating at the same time. He held out his hand and I obediently dropped the key into it.

Inside, the house was dusty, worn, and well used, but not trashed. It would take a few gallons of paint, a kitchen makeover, plumbing and electrical updates, and a lot of elbow grease, but it was doable. As I walked through the rooms, memories of my growing-up years met me with vivid reminders of my past. Most of them were precious and sweet, only a few were painful lessons I'd just as soon remain forgotten.

Wordlessly, Bradley checked all the rooms with either a nod or a shake of his head, mentally and silently listing what had to be done.

"Well?" I prompted when he finished his inspection and stood beside me on the rotting porch.

"Foundation and walls are solid. Roof and porch need replacing. Floors not too bad. A patch here and there, a few pieces of new sheetrock, a little paint, and some updating ought to make it livable again. Got to get rid of this jungle first," he said with a wave of his hand at the kudzu.

"How long will it take?" I asked.

"How long you got?"

I blinked. "I'm renting an apartment for a month. Can this be ready in a month?"

"Maybe, if you're willing to help with the interior."

"Of course. I'd like to help. When can you start?"

"Right now," he said as he took a wicked-looking pair of hedge clippers from his truck.

I sighed. I could see that Bradley was a man of few words. As long as he got the work done, it didn't matter that he couldn't hold a conversation.

I watched for a few minutes as he began clipping vines off at the roots and dragging them away from the house. No use in my staying, I thought. There's nothing I can do to help. I'll go check with Mr. Kirby about a place to stay.

True to his word, Mr. Kirby had a small apartment for me at a very reasonable price. I moved my belongings in and made myself at home. It was clean and adequate. It would do.

When I went back to the house, Bradley had cleared a five-yard space around it, allowing the bones of the building to show. He was a fast but thorough worker and my first impressions of him began to change. We had a short conference about paint colors and what needed to be done first now that the house was free of "the jungle."

We agreed that the roof must be first and then the renovation of the inside. All of it was accomplished with mostly a nod or shake of the head from Bradley, with a few necessary words thrown in when needed. He was obviously intelligent and skilled at his job, but it was highly frustrating to try to talk to him.

Roofers were hired and the work began. I was grateful for the money I had saved from my generous salary. Along with the small amount left in the house account, there was enough to make the place into a home again. It took hours of cleaning to get the inside ready to paint. I did the mopping, scrubbing, and dusting while Bradley fixed broken and missing pieces so skillfully one would hardly know they had ever been less than perfect.

I began to feel that someone was watching the house. Several

63

times, I thought I saw movement at the edge of the wilderness. When I stopped and looked, nothing was there. An animal, I figured. Perhaps a neighbor or youth curious about what's happening to the abandoned property. Or, more likely, just my imagination stirred up by the remarks about the place being haunted.

The day Bradley brought in new cans of paint felt like a milestone and we celebrated. I provided a sack full of brownies from the local bakery and a cooler with beer and sodas to sustain us while Bradley, with a dramatic flourish, brought out new paintbrushes and rollers.

Working together had given us a new level of communication. I learned that Bradley sometimes hummed while he worked, that he was totally focused on what he was doing at the moment, that he didn't appreciate distractions, and that he had a wry sense of humor. Once or twice, I even saw a small smile on his lips when he thought I wasn't watching.

He's also a stickler for perfection. At times, I glimpsed a strict, even harsh, authoritarian who had no qualms about pointing out someone else's lack of skill or careless attention to detail and insist that it's done over. He learned that I was dead serious about reclaiming my house.

As I worked carefully around the windows of a bedroom with my paintbrush, I again saw something move in the edge of the trees. It was very quick, and I watched to see if it was repeated. The second time it happened, I told Bradley.

"There's someone in the trees watching us," I said, trying to hide the nervous catch in my voice.

"Yeah, I saw him. Probably a teenager. Sometimes they dare each other to come to the haunted house. I don't think you have to worry."

Haunted house? The words brought back to mind what both the cab driver and Mr. Kirby said about renters never staying for long. But it's not haunted! I wanted to yell. As I felt the protest coming, I snapped my mouth shut. He's probably right. Why should I be worried? Now that I know what to watch for, I can take a few moans and scares from the local teenagers. They'll find I'm not easy to run off. This is my home. I'm here to stay.

I bought basic furniture and accessories and moved the few things I'd brought from New York into the newly painted rooms. The fragrance of cool, autumn air blending with the lingering smell of new paint was intoxicating, and I couldn't keep the grin off my face.

I used some of the money I saved buying used kitchen appliances instead of new ones to splurge on a good flat-screen TV and Internet connections. Frills would come later. It was enough for now, and I moved myself into the home filled with dreams of my past and hopes for my future.

The first time I heard rustling at the windows and footsteps around the house, I just smiled and went back to sleep. Bradley had seen to it that the locks were strong and the windows sound, so I knew what to expect. They were smart enough not to try every night. Instead, they skipped several nights to make me think they had given up. Then they would be back with new and inventive schemes.

Masked faces would pop up in a window as I entered a room. Sometimes it was a skeleton's head; sometimes a monster with a drooling mouth and long teeth; sometimes a face distorted by a goalie's metal mask, all accompanied by the appropriate sound effects.

It was kid stuff. Teens getting in practice for Halloween, I thought. So far they hadn't damaged anything. I wasn't afraid, but my nerves were getting a bit frazzled. It wasn't until they spray-painted curses on the new front door and cut screens on several windows that I began to be really concerned.

Late one rainy afternoon, I reached my limit. It was a gray day with low clouds, occasional thunder, and a slow, steady rain that left the trees around the house dripping and dismal. I had the car at the garage, so I spent the day puttering. I hung a few pictures, moved furniture around until it suited me, set out the knickknacks that I treasured, trying to make the place look like home. Somehow, it didn't feel right. I couldn't capture the comfortable, safe feeling I remembered in this house.

Finally, I sat at the kitchen window with a cup of tea in the grayness of the rainy day, feeling lonely and depressed, wondering if I had made the biggest mistake of my life in moving back.

That's when I saw him.

At first I thought it was a shadow at the edge of the trees, but when he started moving toward the house, I realized it was a man in a black, hooded raincoat. He must think there's no one here because the car's gone and I hadn't turned on lights.

For a few seconds, I was so stunned I couldn't move. My first thought was that I had no gun, no weapon except the new set of kitchen knives I bought the day before. Sounds of the front door being jimmied forced me to the counter to draw the butcher knife from its slot. I backed up toward the kitchen door, wondering if I should scream for help or just leave. There was no one close enough to hear a scream. I was on my own.

Leave, Rachel, my mind cried. Go while you can!

I knew I should listen, but the aggravations of the past few weeks, the dreariness of the rainy day, and the determination that made me come here in the first place took over. I was not going to give up my house after all the work of fixing it up. I gripped the knife tighter and stood my ground as the new lock on the front door gave way and the door pushed open.

At that moment, a strong arm came around my shoulders, a hand clamped over my mouth, and another hand grasped my arm that held the knife.

"It's okay. It's me," a fierce whisper breathed in my ear.

In the few seconds it took me to realize that "me" was Bradley, I would have collapsed in a puddle of fear if he hadn't been holding me up. He pulled me back into a dark corner of the kitchen, keeping his tight hold on my mouth and my arm. Anger replaced fear, but when I tried to squirm, he turned my head to the side, lifted my chin, moved his hand from my mouth, and instantly covered it again with his lips in a firm, but gentle, kiss.

"Trust me," he whispered, and his hand was back over my mouth.

That did it. Between fear of the intruder and stunned surprise at Bradley being there—not to mention what he just did—my bones seemed to dissolve and my brain spun into neutral, my thoughts so scattered I couldn't think straight. Why is Bradley here? Why should I trust him? Who's breaking into my house? Why? How did Bradley know to be here when they did? How did he get in? I know I locked the doors. What's going on?

Bradley worked his hand up my wrist and took the knife. The intruder was inside, walking softly as he came through the living room into the hall. Just as he reached the kitchen door, he stopped.

Then I heard what he must have heard. A car was coming. I looked away from him to the window and when I looked back, he was gone. He had slipped out like a shadow, and I felt Bradley relax his hold on me.

There was a knock at the door and he whispered, "Go answer it," and gave me a little push.

To my surprise, it was the man from the garage returning my car. A second car idled in the drive, waiting to pick him up. I stood on the porch with my back to the door, hoping he hadn't noticed the marks left by our recent visitor.

"I was on my way home and decided it would be a good time to return your car. She's all fixed and ready to go. We've sent the rental company the bill," he said. "Everything all right out here?"

"Yes, thank you, everything's fine. Thanks for bringing the car and saving me a trip. I appreciate it."

"No problem, Ma'am. We're glad to help."

That's one good reason I've come back, I thought. That sort of kindness would probably never happen in New York. But why did he ask if everything is all right? Does he know what's going on? Did he notice the damage to the door? Or is he just curious about the new resident in the haunted house?

As I went back through the house, I turned on lights to chase the deepening shadows away. Bradley was still waiting in the kitchen.

"Is the door wrecked?" he asked.

"Not too much. It closes, but it won't lock."

"I'll get a new lock," he said and started out.

"Hold it!" I said. "I think I deserve answers to a few things. Someone is breaking into my house; you appear out of nowhere and. . . ."

I sputtered to a stop, took a deep breath, and asked, "How did you get in?"

"I have a key," he said with a hint of a smile on his face.

I stared at him, dumfounded. "Why?"

"I knew you'd need me. I've been here every night."

"How can you be here and I not know it?" I said breathlessly. My lungs didn't seem to work. Nothing made any sense.

"Learned it as a Navy SEAL. They teach sneaking real good."

"Are you a cop?"

"No. I sometimes help them out with surveillance."

"Why am I under surveillance?"

"Not you. The house, and it's a long story. Just know that I'm around most of the time." He moved close to me and caressed my cheek with his fingers. "I care about you, and I don't want anything to happen to you. When this is over, maybe we can get to know each other better."

His touch sent an electric shock through my body. "I think I like you, too," came out of my mouth before I could stop it. I was stunned, but rewarded. He smiled—a genuine, warm smile that transformed his stern face into something quite different and very appealing.

I stared like an idiot and by the time I got my mouth closed, he was gone.

The week before Halloween, the visits from the masked youths increased. Sleep was ripped away each night by the inventive sounds and weird happenings they conjured up, and I began to understand why no renter had stayed very long.

I spoke to the local police, and they all but laughed at me. They would speak to the kids, they said, but nothing changed. The police department was very small, some of those kids were theirs, and since no one was hurt, no serious damage was done, they didn't think it necessary to waste their time on it. I could either wait it out or leave as everyone else had. The intruder they dismissed as just a bolder kid.

The only thing that held me together was knowing that Bradley was nearby. He was around during the day painting the outside of the house. I seldom saw him at night, but I could feel his presence. When thunderstorms rumbled overhead, I sensed he was inside, in the spare bedroom, and I didn't care. I didn't look. All I felt was glad that he was there and not out in the storm. I still didn't understand what was going on, why someone was so determined to drive me out of my house, why I needed a protector, and why the police didn't simply throw the kids in jail and put a stop to it.

Then on Halloween night it all became clear.

Bradley came in mid-afternoon.

"I think tonight will be the end of your troubles here, but you have to help. Everyone needs to believe you're gone and the house is empty. Turn out the lights and stay in your room. Don't come out no matter what you hear. Trust me. This will all be over soon."

Then he was gone.

Trust me. Well, I was learning it was okay to trust him, but if it wasn't over soon I was going to demand some answers.

I did as he said and much later, I understood what the word cower meant. Still dressed, I huddled under the covers, listening with all my senses. At first, I barely heard the soft footsteps; the quiet thumps of furniture being moved. With the first sound of ripping wallboard, I almost sprang out of bed. He's tearing up my house! Why doesn't Bradley stop him?

A few pounds of a hammer, the shriek of sheetrock and wood being pried apart, and then quiet except for a shuffling noise.

Suddenly, there was an explosion of sounds.

A man's scream. Muttered curses. The wail of sirens. More thumps and scuffling sounds. Flashing red and blue lights streaming into the yard.

I made it out of bed and out the door before I lost my nerve. The living room light was on; Bradley was sitting on top of someone facedown on the floor; police were coming through the front door with guns drawn. They handcuffed the man on the floor and jerked him to his feet. He looked at me with shock and I remembered him as one of the roofers as they hustled him out to the waiting police car. Bradley and I stared at each other over a gaping hole in my wall. The police car drove off with their suspect, leaving a deputy on guard.

When I looked into that hole, I nearly fainted with surprise. It was full of money! Bags of it! Suddenly, I understood. I had been used as bait to catch a thief.

I looked at Bradley. He saw the anger and the questions in my eyes and looked away.

"Why?" I said through clenched teeth.

"They suspected this guy was guilty of dozens of robberies and dope dealing, but they could never find the evidence to convict him. Clever fellow never had any excess money on him. Last month, one of the kids who 'haunted' the house let slip he expected 'business to pick up soon.'

"Our thief hired the kids to scare people away from the house so he could use it to hide his loot. When you moved in and started renovating, he knew he had to get his stash out. It was necessary that he lead us to the money to make a conviction stick, so we wanted him to think you'd gone for the night and the house was empty. Might be the last chance to get his money, if it was really there. I hid your car back in the woods. "

"You are a cop," I said bitterly.

"No. It's like I said. I only help out now and then."

"So helping with the house, protecting me, was just a set-up. None of it was real?"

He moved close to me. "Started out like that. I wanted it to stay that way, but I began to care about you. We connected in a way I never have with a woman before. You're different. Not flirty and teasing, just down-to-earth and genuine. Something my heart truly needs."

My own heart was thumping so hard I could hardly breathe. I stared at him, trying to re-gather the anger that had quickly scattered. The deputy left to guard the money grinned and stepped out onto the porch.

Bradley took my face in his hands. "This part is very real," he said softly and kissed me gently.

As before, my bones seemed to melt and I returned his kiss. He lifted his head long enough to smile that wonderful smile and then repeated the kiss, only sweeter, stronger. I leaned into him and it felt right. There was much I still needed to know about this man, but all the doubts about coming back suddenly became very small.

Whatever the problems were, I'm home.

THE END

A 6-YEAR-OLD HAUNTS
MY HOUSE

I'll never forget the first day we moved into the house. I'd been through a terrible divorce, forced out of my beautiful home, and had to go back to work. Austin and I were all on our own now. Allen had won everything in the courts. His lawyer proved that Allen had brought everything into the family and made all the money while we were married. He had also cast doubt that Austin was Allen's son.

Brokenhearted, we'd left the courtroom demoralized and broke. The only money I was allowed to keep was some my grandmother left me in a trust. I'd been saving it for Austin's college, but we needed it now.

I turned the car down the lane leading to the little house sitting among tall oaks. It looked so peaceful, and a sob caught in my throat. We hadn't had much peace in so long and we could use some now. But I knew there wasn't time for just relaxing. Our furniture would be arriving tomorrow, bright and early, and the place was a mess. The realtor told me nobody had lived in the house for two years. Its unlikely name was Birchwood. Not because the place had any birch trees but because the family who built the house was named Birch.

Austin got out of the car without a word. He stood staring at the house a long time, then stomped sullenly toward the little front porch.

"Austin," I called. "Come help me with the cleaning stuff." I began to pull bags from the car trunk.

He returned, still without saying a word. I knew he was hurt and feeling resentful, but we had to get the house in shape for our furniture. The house had three small bedrooms and a bathroom on the upper floor and kitchen, living room, and bath on the first floor. It was deplorable considering what we'd just moved from, but I couldn't think about that now.

Austin will adjust, I told myself.

We started upstairs and worked our way down. By noon we had the bedrooms and baths sparkling clean and were ready to start on the rooms downstairs. Austin hadn't said a word, but he'd worked hard. My heart overflowed with love for this twelve-year-old who'd gotten caught in a nasty divorce case. None of it was his fault, but he had to pay just the same.

Austin was born six months after Allen and I married. Allen knew very well Austin was his because we'd been dating for six months and I'd never dated anyone but him. I was so crazy in love with him that I'd agreed to have sex, hoping I'd get pregnant. Allen was a handsome man, well-built with a devastating smile. When I told him I was pregnant, he said, "Well, I guess we'd better plan on getting married." I thought it meant I would spend the rest of my life with him. Oh, how wrong I'd been.

I had no inkling that Allen was dissatisfied with our marriage until a few months ago. I'd always been a stay-at-home mom, enjoying every minute. We had a beautiful home, a beautiful son, and a perfect marriage.

When he told me he was moving out and wanted a divorce, I screamed and cried and tried to convince him that we loved each other and whatever problems we had, we could work them out. He never heard me, just kept packing his bag and telling me his plans. The house would be sold. I could keep my car and could take what furniture I wanted. I never realized he wasn't going to pay alimony or child support until we went to court.

My lawyer was as surprised as me when Allen's lawyer stated Austin was not his child, therefore he would pay no child support. I sat stunned as Allen testified that I wasn't a good wife and refused to get a job, even after Austin started school. Nobody reminded him that it was his idea that I stay at home. He wanted his dinner on time and his house warm and inviting when he came home. I was crying so hard when it was all over. I stumbled from the courthouse and out to my car.

When Austin asked how it went, I told him the truth. Looking back, I realize I could've softened the blow, but I was too confused and scared to think about his needs.

Things moved fast after that. Allen sold the house, so we had to move. I'd found this little place as soon as possible and we were preparing to move in.

"Let's stop and fix a sandwich," I told Austin. We made our sandwiches, took our cold drinks, and went out to sit on the front steps. A small squirrel ran across the yard and scampered up a tree. I couldn't help but smile, but Austin silently chewed his sandwich.

I felt I had to say something. "No matter what happens, Austin, please know that I love you very much and I'll do everything I can to make you happy."

"Then make Dad love me again," he said, a catch in his voice.

I swallowed. "Believe me, I would if I could, darling," I said, patting him on his leg.

"Doesn't matter," he said, flinging his sandwich across the yard. "I hate him. I hope he dies tomorrow."

"No you don't, dear. Hating will make you a bitter person, and then your father would have ruined both our lives."

"Maybe you don't think our lives are ruined, living in this shack, walking half a mile to the bus, having the kids laugh at me at school. If you ask me, it's not much of a life."

I winced. What good would it do to tell him I was doing the best I could? He was so wrapped up in his own misery that he couldn't understand anything else.

But I couldn't help but mutter, "I'm doing the best I can. Come on, let's go into our shack and finish cleaning. The furniture will be here tomorrow."

My heart ached for him as I followed his dejected figure into the house. That night we slept in sleeping bags on the floor. Sometime during the night I awoke to the sound of Austin sobbing. I wanted to go to him but I knew he would be ashamed. He was at the age when boys don't cry but keep a stiff upper lip.

Morning dawned clear and cool. With the movers came a surprise. Allen's parents were right behind them. I hadn't seen them since the split, and I didn't know what to think about them being there.

Maggie never said a word, just folded me in her arms and hugged me close. Ralph wrapped his arms around Austin's shoulders and patted him on the shoulder. "How you doing, boy?" he asked gruffly.

"Fine, I guess," Austin said. He'd always loved his grandparents, but he didn't know how to respond to them now.

"Why don't we get inside and tell these movers where you want this furniture placed," Maggie said briskly as she led the way. Maggie had always been a take-charge woman with a warm and giving heart. But, like Austin, I didn't know what to say to them now. Ralph carried a large paper bag which he deposited on the kitchen counter.

"Maggie insisted we bring breakfast because you might not have anything to cook on." He began pulling bacon and egg sandwiches from the bag. They smelled wonderful and I realized we hadn't eaten much since we'd arrived. He poured orange juice for Austin and coffee for me.

We stood munching on the delicious sandwiches as the men moved our furniture in. Maggie and I supervised the placing of it while Ralph and Austin had another sandwich.

I couldn't help but wonder what Allen's parents thought about this poor little house compared to their elegant home. Ralph was a very successful lawyer and his son had followed in his footsteps.

When the furniture was in place and the movers left, Maggie suggested we rest a few minutes before we started unpacking the boxes. We moved into the living room in awkward silence.

"I won't beat around the bush," Ralph said, dropping down beside Austin. "I think it is appalling what Allen has done to his family. I only found out yesterday that he hadn't provided for you. No alimony and no child support."

"He said I wasn't his child," Austin said, struggling to keep back the tears.

Ralph put his arm around him and pulled him close. "Of course you're his son," he said. "Which makes you my grandson." Austin buried his head in Ralph's side and let the tears come. "There, there," said Ralph. "Things are going to work out. Let's talk about it."

"There's nothing to talk about," I said. "Allen's lawyer said because I didn't bring anything into the marriage, didn't contribute to the income, and Austin was not Allen's son, we weren't entitled to anything." I still ached with hurt as I remembered the hateful words.

"And did anybody suggest a DNA test for Austin?"

"I didn't have the money and Allen said it didn't take a DNA test to prove anything to him."

"And what did he say about how much the boy looks like him?" Maggie said quietly.

"He didn't mention it," I told her.

"Well, first things first," Ralph said. "Let's get this unpacking done and then I'll treat everybody to a steak dinner. Tomorrow I want you both at my office bright and early. I'll have everything set up for a DNA test for Austin and we'll move to have the contents of the divorce papers set aside, proving how much you contributed to the marriage even though it wasn't monetary."

Tears sprang to my eyes. "Why are you doing this?"

"Because we think Allen is acting like a spoiled brat and we have no intention of losing our grandson because of his selfishness. You must know how much we love you and Austin," said Maggie, rising to her feet and hugging us both. "Now let's get these boxes unpacked and put away. A big, juicy steak sounds good to me."

We worked most of the day getting things in shape. Maggie and Ralph worked as hard as we did, encouraging Austin and telling him stories about when they were young and started married life in a two-room apartment. Ralph had Austin laughing before the afternoon was over. And the steaks did taste wonderful.

Driving home, Austin chatted happily about his grandparents. I realized how much he was afraid of losing them if they turned against him, too. He looked and acted like his old self.

We went to bed early and I fell asleep immediately, so grateful for the Fords and their offer to help. I was awakened about two o'clock by the sound of sobbing. I couldn't believe my ears. Austin had been so happy when we'd said good night. But apparently it had all been a front. He sobbed as if his heart would break. The sobbing stopped after thirty minutes, but I lay awake the rest of the night.

"Morning, Mom," Austin said cheerfully as he entered the kitchen the next morning. "What's for breakfast? Pancakes, I hope."

"Pancakes it is," I said, looking closely at him. His eyes were clear and his smile was warm.

He ate his pancakes silently and headed back upstairs to change. Troubled, I stood at the sink, looking out over the unkempt yard. Another thing I'd have to take care of. The weight on my heart settled back in and I struggled with how to comfort my son.

As I drove the short distance to town, I tried to make conversation, but Austin seemed distracted. "Are you okay, son?" I asked.

"Sure, Mom," he said. He turned to look directly at me. "I want to tell you that I believe things are going to be okay with Grandma and Grandpa helping us."

"I think so, too," I said softly.

"Does that mean you won't cry anymore at night?"

"Cry anymore?" I asked, puzzled.

"Yeah," he said, suddenly embarrassed. "I heard you crying the last two nights."

"You heard me crying." I gasped. "I heard it, too. I thought it was you."

"It wasn't me," he said. We turned to stare at each other. If it wasn't either of us, then who was it?

I didn't for a minute believe Austin would lie. He'd just never gotten into the habit.

We parked in front of Ralph's office and went in. His secretary greeted us warmly and ushered us immediately into Ralph's spacious office. The next hour was spent answering questions and going over paperwork. The phone on the desk buzzed and Ralph said, "Send her in."

"This is Alma," he said of the young woman who entered. "Alma is going to do the DNA test for us. Would you go in the next room with her, Austin?"

In a few minutes they were back and Ralph got up and escorted us through the outer office and onto the sidewalk. "Go home and do whatever you can to live as normally as possible. Do you need money?"

Tears rushed to my eyes again. "We're all right for now, Ralph. I thank you for trying to help us, but Allen is going to be awfully mad."

"Allen's father is already mad," he said, ruffling Austin's hair. "I'll not forgive him easily for trying to take our grandson away."

We didn't talk much on the way home. We worked together finishing up our unpacking and doing our rooms. A new bicycle was delivered in the middle of the afternoon. From Grandma to Austin the card read. Austin was pleased beyond words and went immediately to call his grandma. I just stood staring at the shiny new bike, tears blinding me. We were going to be fine.

Austin went off down the road on his new bike and I stayed home washing clothes and getting my clothes ready to start my new job on Monday. It wasn't a fancy job, but it would pay our bills. I would be working as a clerk in the largest department store in town.

The work was hard and I was tired when I got home. One reason was the sobbing in the house woke me almost every night. Sunday night I decided to find the culprit, halfway believing it was Austin.

I padded across the hall to his room and looked in. He lay on his side, eyes open.

"Do you hear it, too, Mom?" he whispered.

"Yes," I said. "It sounds as if it is coming from this room."

"Sounds to me like it's coming from your room." He was right. Now that I was in his room, the sobs were coming from my room.

"What are we going to do, Mom?"

I could tell by his voice that he was afraid. "I don't know, son. Why don't I sleep with you the rest of the night and we'll talk about it tomorrow."

He didn't argue as I slipped into bed beside him. Soon the sobbing stopped and we both slept.

There was no time to discuss it the next morning. Austin had to catch the school bus and I had to start my job. I hugged him hard and told him I loved him.

Maggie came by the job that day. She'd purchased clothes for Austin and asked if she could bring him to her house after school and let me pick him up after work. "That way, he won't have to be home by himself."

I shivered, thinking of him going home by himself, so I gratefully accepted her offer.

And so we settled into a routine. The job went well but it was tiring. By the time we got home we were tired. After a quick supper we watched some television then went to bed. If Austin heard the sobbing again he never mentioned it, but I heard it. I walked all over the house trying to find the source, but it was always just ahead of me or just behind me.

One night as we finished supper, we heard a car outside.

"It's Dad," said Austin, moving toward the back door.

I waited for his knock and opened the door. He'd never looked more handsome, but there was a scowl on his face. "I want to talk to you," he said.

I stepped past him and onto the little porch. I didn't want him in the house.

"I thought we had an understanding about the divorce. You know everything my attorney said in court was true. You didn't earn a penny when we were married and I doubt if Austin is mine."

"He's yours, Allen," I said, dropping into the rickety porch swing. "And you know it."

He looked surprised. I'd never argued with him before. "You were pregnant when we married, therefore it could be anybody's."

Suddenly, I was sick of the sight of him. "Say what you came to say and go," I told him.

"I've been served with a subpoena ordering me to have a DNA test. Also, ordering a new hearing to see if you deserve alimony. You won't win this one either, Emily. You're wasting your time and money."

"Time and money is something I have plenty of," I snapped, getting to my feet. "If you're finished, please go."

"How dare you drag my parents into this. I hoped you would be honorable enough to settle this between us."

"Why don't you talk to your father, Allen, not me. I have no idea what's going on. You mother asked to keep her grandson after school and I took her up on the offer so he wouldn't have to be home by himself. In case you're interested, he's doing fine."

"I want you to leave my parents out of this," he threatened. He stomped off the porch and into his car. The gravel spurted under his wheels as he left.

I went into the house and called Ralph. "Allen just left. He was very angry. Said I should leave you all out of this mess."

"The next time he calls or comes, tell him to speak to your lawyer. He didn't harm you, did he?"

"No," I said wearily. I was tempted to leave the dishes until tomorrow. "Just yelled at me."

"Don't worry," he said. "He won't come back. I'll see to it."

"Thank you," I said, going into the kitchen where Austin was busily drying the dishes he'd had already washed. I hugged him close, letting the tears flow. He never asked what his father wanted. I had a feeling he'd listened at the door.

Summer came and school was out. Austin never objected to staying home by himself, but he was always outside when I came home. One afternoon, he came rushing out to meet me.

"Mom, I got a job. I got a job for the summer."

"That's wonderful, dear," I said, trying to figure out what we were having for dinner. "Who's giving you a job?"

"Robert Brooks. He lives on the next farm. He has horses and everything. He said he needed help around the place in the summer."

"How did you meet Mr. Brooks?"

"I was riding my bike and slid into the ditch. He was working across the fence and he came and helped me up. We got to talking and he asked if I liked horses. I told him I didn't know much about them but I liked them. He asked if I'd like to see his and I said yes. Mom, he has a bunch. He raises them for race tracks. He said I could help him around the barn."

"Why don't we go see Mr. Brooks before I give my permission?"

"Okay," he said, racing out to the car. I hadn't seen him this excited in a long time.

We drove further down the blacktop road that ran in front of our house. I'd never been any further than our lane.

A line of trees separated Birchwood from the Brooks farm. The house sat back from the road, down a tree-lined road. It was green and well kept, lawns mowed and buildings painted.

We drove past the house to a corral where a man was working with a horse. He turned and walked toward us as I stopped and Austin got out. "Hey, Robert," he called. "I brought my mom."

"Hello, Mrs. Ford," he said, offering his hand. His smile was friendly and he was tanned from working in the sun. His hand was rough and callused. I judged him to be about my age.

"Hello, Mr. Brooks," I said. "Austin tells me you want him to work for you this summer. I thought I'd better come by and make sure all he said was true."

"It's true," he said, smiling as he watched Austin climb on the fence and pat the beautiful horse's neck. "He's a great kid."

"Yes, he is," I agreed.

I followed him as he walked toward the fence, explaining Austin's chores. "He'll be doing clean-up in the barn, shoveling fertilizer, and feeding the animals. I might teach him to ride if you have no objections."

I knew I couldn't object, although I had a scared feeling in the pit of my stomach as I pictured Austin on the back of one of those big horses.

"If you're sure he won't be in the way."

"Not at all." He smiled up at Austin. "Looks like I got myself a new hand for the summer, son." He patted Austin on the back and swung up beside him.

I listened to them chatting together and wished with all my heart that his dad would take half as much interest. When Austin ran off to see the barn, Robert Brooks turned to me.

"Sorry I haven't gotten by to see you since you moved in. Guess I'm not a very good neighbor. When my wife was alive she took care of things like that. I guess I have a lot to learn. How do you like the old Birchwood house?"

"It's fine," I said. "It's a nice, solid house."

"I'll come over tomorrow and do your lawn. Austin said you hadn't gotten anyone to do it since you moved in."

"That's very kind of you," I said. "But I'm sure we'll be able to get it done."

"It's the only way I know to be a good neighbor. I don't bake." We both laughed and it felt good. "Why don't you leave Austin here? I'll bring him home in time for supper."

"Only if you'll have supper with us," I heard myself saying. I blushed to the roots of my hair, but he didn't seem to notice.

"Sounds like a deal to me."

I was nervous as I prepared supper, putting out my best dishes and making sure everything was neat and clean. I knew the house was no mansion, but it suited me.

Supper was pleasant and we didn't have to worry about any awkward moments because Austin chatted constantly. Right in the middle of a conversation, Austin blurted out something about the sobbing we'd heard.

"Mom thought it was me and I thought it was her," he said. "But when we got together, we could still hear it."

Nobody spoke for a long moment, then Robert spoke.

"I believe I'd like a little more of that roast, Austin."

Austin didn't seem to notice that Robert Brooks hadn't reacted to his statement.

When Austin finished and carried his plate to the sink, Robert said, "I'll help your mother with the dishes, son. Why don't you go watch a little television, if it's all right with your mother?"

"Cool," Austin said, and scooted out of the room.

"I'll wash and you dry," he said, rinsing out the sink. "You know where everything goes."

He seemed to know his way around the kitchen and seemed to be comfortable. It fleetingly crossed my mind that I'd never seen Allen with a dish towel in his hands.

"You want to tell me about the crying Austin mentioned?" he said, glancing over his shoulder to make sure Austin was out of earshot.

I hesitated. Would he think I was crazy?

"When the Channings lived here, Mike talked of a child crying sometimes. His wife couldn't stand it, so they moved away. I guess they still owned the house when you bought it."

"Channings?" I said. "I believe they were the former owners. You say they heard a child crying? I wonder why the real estate lady didn't say anything."

"Probably wanted to sell this place real bad."

"Yes, and I imagine that's why the price was so low."

He let the water out of the sink and rinsed the dishcloth. "She may not have known their reason for leaving or she could be new in the neighborhood. I don't think the Channings discussed the problem with anybody but me, and I never discussed it. Debbie got sick about that time and for the next two years, we concentrated on her." His eyes looked haunted. I knew he'd loved his wife and missed her.

"I'm sorry about your wife."

"Thank you," he said. "She was a wonderful woman."

For just a moment I felt envy. No man had ever spoken about me with that kind of love.

"Have you heard anything except the crying?"

"No," I said. "But it's so sad."

He stuck his head in the den and told Austin good-bye, telling him he'd see him tomorrow. I walked him out to his pickup and we stood looking back at the house.

"Did you know who lived here before the Channings?"

"Oh, yes. The Halfords bought it from the Birches after Mr. Birch passed away. His wife passed away about a year before him. They built the house, you know. They were there when my father bought the horse ranch." He reached for the handle of his truck. "I'm not far away, so call me if you need me. Austin has my number." He touched my shoulder lightly and got in his truck and drove away.

Austin was ecstatic at being able to work for Robert. When I came home the next afternoon, the lawn was cut and trimmed, with dead limbs piled against the fence. Tears rushed to my eyes as I hurried into the house to answer a ringing phone.

"Hi, it's me," Ralph said. "I have some good news today. The judge set aside the decision not to pay you child support for Austin. He awarded you three hundred a month. The checks will come here and I will forward them."

"Oh, Ralph!" I cried. "How can I thank you?" I stood in the foyer talking on the phone. A movement caught my eye and I looked up the stairs. On the top landing a young girl stood. She was dressed in a checked pinafore and white blouse. She wore white socks and patent leather shoes. She looked to be about six years old. Her eyes were so sad and she looked directly at me. As I stared she began to fade away, then she was gone. I gasped.

"Emily, are you okay?" Ralph asked.

"Ralph," I blurted out before I could stop myself. "I think I just saw a ghost."

"You saw a what?" he almost shouted.

Taking a deep breath, I tried to quiet my pounding heart. "I'm sorry, Ralph," I said. "What were you saying?"

"Forgot what I was saying. What were you saying?"

"It's a long story, Ralph."

"Well, I've got all the time in the world."

So I told him about the crying child we'd both heard during the night. "I think the child I saw was the one we hear."

"Emily, is Austin there?"

"No, he's working for Mr. Brooks who owns a horse ranch right next to us. He loves it and Mr. Brooks seems so nice."

"In case you're wondering why I'm not surprised to hear what you said, my wife told me Austin told her about hearing a child cry in the house. She didn't want to believe him so she changed the subject. Why don't we make arrangements to get you and Austin out of that house?"

"I don't think so, Ralph," I said slowly. "I believe she was asking me for help. She isn't a threat. I don't know how I know that, but I really believe she wants me to help her."

"Help her do what?" Ralph asked.

"I don't know, Ralph, but I want to stay here and try."

"Okay," he said slowly, "but if you need help, don't hesitate to call me. And one more thing. If we have to have a hearing on whether or not Allen owes you for all the time you put in keeping his house, raising his child, and doing all the hundred and one things all wives do, you'll have to testify. I may be able to convince him without using you."

"I don't know how to thank you, Ralph," I said. "You and your wife. You have been so kind to us."

"Can't take the chance of losing my grandson," he said gruffly and hung up the phone.

I never mentioned the image to Austin, but I never looked up the stairs without expecting to see her there.

Maggie called me Thursday night. "How about Ralph and I come out and spend the weekend? We haven't seen either of you in so long."

"Oh, Maggie," I said. "I'm sorry I haven't had time to bring Austin by, but we've both been so busy."

"I understand," she said kindly. "Can we come?"

"You're welcome to," I said, my mind racing. "Austin can sleep on his sleeping bag in my room and you and Ralph can have his bed. Would that be okay?" I knew they were coming because of the ghost I'd seen.

"That would be fine. Don't fix supper. We'll pick something up on the way."

Austin was ecstatic about seeing his grandparents. He spent the first hour telling them all about Robert Brooks and how much fun it was to work at his ranch. His eyes shone and he laughed at his own funny stories.

"Looks like you've become a regular cowboy," Ralph teased, looking at the brand-new cowboy boots Austin had bought with his first paycheck. "Well, I brought something you might like." They left the table together for Ralph to show Austin the cowboy hat he'd brought him.

"He's a fine boy," Maggie said with tears in her eyes as we began to clear the table. "I understand Ralph forced Allen to pay child support for his son. I'm sorry it had to be that way, but Allen has turned out to be a great disappointment to us. He's getting married again, you know."

"No, I didn't know," I said, turning away.

"Emily," she said, putting her hand on my arm. "I don't want you to worry about Austin's college education. Ralph and I are going to see to it."

Suddenly I was crying. She held me in her arms and patted me on the shoulder.

When things had quieted down, she brought up the subject that had brought them to our house. "Have you seen the little girl again?"

"No," I said, "but sometimes I think I can feel her presence. She's so sad, Maggie. I wish I could help her."

"Maybe you can," she sighed. "What kind of help do you think she needs?"

"I don't know. I just don't know."

"Hey, you guys going to come watch TV? A good movie is on." Ralph stood smiling at us from the doorway. "Austin said popcorn wouldn't be bad."

We spent the next two hours enjoying a movie and eating popcorn. We were all a little nervous as we went up to bed, but nothing happened to interrupt our sleep.

Austin and Ralph went over to the Brooks ranch bright and early the next morning while Maggie and I did the dishes, then went to town shopping for lunch and dinner.

We invited Robert Brooks over for a cookout. Everybody had a wonderful time. Austin decided to go in and watch some TV. We were having coffee on the back patio when Ralph brought up the subject of our ghost.

"What do you know about the history of this house?" he asked Robert.

"Not a whole lot. The Birches owned it when my dad bought the ranch. They both passed away while I was in college. The Halfords bought the place and lived there about five years. Then the Channings moved in, but didn't stay long."

"Did the Channings have children?" Ralph asked.

"I don't believe so. I think they were newlyweds."

"And the Halfords, did they have children?"

"I don' t know, but we could ask my mother. She always knew

81

the neighbors much better than me. After Debbie and I married and moved to the ranch, we were pretty busy. Dad had been sick the last few years and the place needed a lot of work." His voice trailed off and we could tell he was remembering his wife.

"I understand your wife is dead," Maggie said.

"Yes. She had breast cancer and went so fast we hardly had time to realize what the problem was."

Maggie patted him on the arm and moved to go in the house. Robert said he'd better say good-bye to Austin. "I had a good time. Thanks for the invitation."

We all walked him to the car and then watched TV. We were all in the bed by ten-thirty and I went to sleep almost immediately. At two-thirty Austin was shaking my shoulder.

"Mom," he said. "Mom, wake up. It's doing it again."

Awakened, I sat up in bed and listened. He was right. It was happening again. We opened the door to the hall and found Maggie and Ralph standing in the doorway, looking down the hall toward the bath.

"I think it's coming from the bathroom," Maggie whispered. She and Ralph started that way. Austin and I didn't move. We knew when they got there it would start coming from some other place.

As they opened the bathroom door, the sobbing began in the room across the hall. "It's never where you think it is," whispered Austin as they came back. He motioned toward his bedroom and they went in. Again the sobbing stopped for a second, then began in the extra bedroom. Ralph started down the short hallway with purposeful steps.

"Won't do any good, Grandpa. It'll move again."

And it did, but this time we couldn't tell where it was coming from because now it was all round us. Ralph motioned to us and we all went down the stairs. As we reached the bottom floor, the sobbing stopped completely.

"Strangest thing I ever heard," said Ralph, scratching his head.

We made coffee and talked about the phenomenon. Austin fell asleep and Ralph and Maggie began to discuss us getting away from this place.

"I can't move," I said. "I've put all our extra money in this house and furthermore, I believe the little girl needs help. I know that sounds crazy, but that's the way I feel."

They finally agreed. "But if you ever feel in danger, please call us."

The rest of the weekend went by without incident. My in-laws went home early Monday morning and I went back to work. Austin went back to the Brooks ranch. I'd told Maggie and Ralph that I would talk to Austin about how he felt.

My phone was ringing when I came home that night. "Hi, Emily.

It's Robert. If you have time you can come over and talk to my mother. She knows more about the people who've lived in your house."

Mrs. Brooks was a lively little woman with gray hair and sparkling blue eyes. It was obvious she loved her son and was pleased to have Austin around.

"Mom," he said, "this is Emily, Austin's mother. As I told you, they live in the old Birch house and they've had some unusual experiences. She needs any information you can give her."

"Sit down, Emily," she said, waving her hand at a couch across from her. Robert slipped quietly from the room.

"Robert tells me you're interested in the people who lived at Birchwood. The Birches built the house. They bought the acreage from the man who owned this place. They sold it back to us when we bought the ranch because they were no longer able to raise their vegetables. You see, they raised vegetables to sell to the local merchants. Mr. Birch had a heart attack and died. Mrs. Birch sold the house to the Halfords. Mr. Halford was a big, blustery man who was always causing trouble with his neighbors. His wife was a meek little thing and I always believed he abused her. Right after they moved in, her niece came to live with them. Mrs. Halford said Mr. Halford wasn't too happy about it, but she had no place else to go. I only saw her a few times. She seemed to be a sweet little thing. About six years old, I think. Mrs. Halford brought her here a few times and I used to see her in the yard when I passed. Her name was Layla.

"The Halfords moved abruptly one night. We never knew why. I was surprised because Judy Halford and I were just beginning to get acquainted. Her husband went on trips frequently and she'd come over and bring the little girl. She would get nervous after she'd been here a while and hurry back, saying she was afraid Marty might come home unexpectedly. My husband tried to be neighborly with Marty Halford, but he wasn't interested.

"The house stayed empty a couple of years and then the Channings moved in. They were a sweet couple, newly married. They did a lot of work on the house and yard. At first Mrs. Channing loved the house, then she began to talk about strange goings on there. When I pressed her, she said strange noises. They moved out without selling. Moved to town, I believe. I think they're still there. I believe they have one child now."

"Did the Birches have any children?"

"No. I think Mr. Birch was sterile. Something that happened to him when he was in the war. They had several animals but no children."

We talked a few more minutes, then I went to find Robert.

"Did you get anything you can use?" he asked.

"Yes," I replied. "She knew that the Halfords were the only ones who lived in the house with a small child. A niece, I believe. They left suddenly without telling anyone where they were going. They weren't very friendly, so your mother didn't think too much about it. Said Mr. Halford was an unpleasant man and his wife was a timid little thing who was afraid of him."

"I'm glad she could help," he said, walking beside me as I went to my car. "How about I bring Austin home and take you both to a movie later?"

He was so nice and friendly, I couldn't refuse.

Five days later Austin brought home a puppy that someone had thrown out at the Brooks ranch. "Robert said he'd help me build a dog house and pen if you'd let me keep him. Can I?"

How could I refuse? He hadn't been so excited about anything in a long time, and I have to admit he was a cute little thing. He scurried all around the kitchen exploring every corner. Austin fed him from his plate and played with him until it was time to go to bed. He picked the dog up and started up the stairs with him. The dog began to wiggle and bark. When Austin sat him down at the head of the stairs he started down, but the steps were too steep and he tumbled the rest of the way. When Austin tried to take him up again, he wiggled out of his arms and ran to the farthest corner and refused to come out.

We finally gave up and fixed him a bed in the kitchen. In the next few days, we tried to coax him upstairs, but he refused to go. He would stand at the bottom of the steps and growl menacingly up the stairs, but he wouldn't go up.

Robert, true to his word, came over to help Austin with the dog house and pen. They drew up plans and laid out the space for the pen. We were tired that Saturday and went to bed early. Ruff, which was Austin's name for the dog, still refused to go up the stairs.

It was about two in the morning when I felt Austin shaking my shoulder. "Mom," he whispered. "Come see."

"Come see what?"

"Just come see," he insisted, leading the way out of my room and across the hall to his. He walked to the window and pulled back the curtain. "Look," he said.

It was a bright, moonlit night and the backyard was well-lit. But Austin was pointing to the corner of the yard. A small girl stood there looking up toward the window. I gasped. It was the same little girl I'd seen at the top of the stairs. As we stared at her, she disappeared.

"Did you see that?" Austin whispered. "She's been standing there a long time. I spotted her when I let Ruff out. So when I came back up here, I looked out and she was still there. You could see right through her. It was like she was looking right at me."

"Yes," I said. "I've seen her before. Austin, I think she wants us to help her."

"What does she want us to do?" he asked.

"I don't know, son," I said. "She looked so sad and I'm sure she's the one we hear crying." I hugged him close and put him back to bed. I walked slowly back to my room. Was the little girl trying to tell us something? I didn't sleep much the rest of the night.

Robert was back over Sunday afternoon. Ruff was in the yard with the two, frisking around as if he knew all their energies were focusing on something. Suddenly, I heard him barking furiously. I stepped out on the back porch to take the boys some lemonade.

"What's the matter with Ruff?"

"Don't know," said Austin. "He's been acting funny ever since we've come out. He goes over to the corner of the yard and starts barking, then he begins to dig. He's acting crazy."

"Isn't that where we saw the little girl the other night?" I asked, setting the pitcher and glasses on the porch table. I walked toward the spot where the dog stood.

"What little girl?" Robert asked, straightening up from his job.

"We saw what looked like the ghost of a little girl over there."

All three of us walked over to where the dog was acting up. He'd tried to dig up the dirt but it was too hard. He ran back and forth across the same spot, barking loudly.

"Austin," said Robert solemnly. "Why don't you bring me a shovel. Let's see what is making this dog so excited."

A cold chill ran up my spine as I looked at the spot. It seemed to be no different than the rest of the yard, but suddenly it was cold in this shady spot.

The shovel cut the dirt and Robert lifted out a shovel full. Without looking up, he continued. I don't think any of us were surprised when the shovel struck something besides dirt. It was something in a plastic bag. We knew even before we opened it that it was the body of a small girl. She was dressed in a blue checked apron and had long hair.

"Call the police, Austin," Robert said, stepping between Austin and the pitiful sight on the ground. He put his arms around me and held me close as I began to sob. I felt as if I knew this child, buried in an unmarked grave in a plastic bag.

The police came, took our statements, and took the body away. They promised they would look in to a possible homicide. The sergeant said it looked like she'd died from a blow on the head.

"I want you two to come home with me," Robert said, his arm still around me. "You can't stay here tonight." We both agreed.

I couldn't stop shaking. That little girl I'd seen had been murdered. If she'd died a natural death, they wouldn't have hidden

85

her. Robert stayed close by, even sitting with me on the couch all night talking about little things to distract my attention. I think that was the time I began falling in love with him.

We went home to stay a few days later and things settled into the old routine—except there was no more crying at night and I never saw the little girl's ghost again. Ruff ran up and down the steps and the house seemed much more friendly. Robert is a frequent visitor and Austin's grandparents come by every Sunday after church.

The sheriff came by one day to tell us they'd caught the Halfords in Alabama. After they arrested Marty Halford, Mrs. Halford gave them all the grisly details. Marty Halford was a real prince. He'd molested the little girl and when she fought back, he'd killed her. He threatened the same for Mrs. Halford if she ever told. I was so glad Mr. Halford would pay for his crime, but most of all I'm glad Layla is finally at rest.

It's summer again and Austin has grown at least six inches. Ruff is a fine watchdog and Robert and I plan to marry in the fall. He is a wonderful man and will make a fine husband and a good father.

THE END

DRACULA IS
MY BABY'S DADDY
I don't know how to tell my husband.

I wasn't certain about my outfit, so I anxiously asked my best friend, Isabelle, "You don't think it's too revealing?" Isabelle and her husband, Matthew, lived next door.

I self-consciously yanked at the bodice of the ridiculously low-cut peasant blouse. The top of the blouse barely covered my nipples!

Isabelle sat on the bed, laughing at my antics. "Honey, you've got the bust for it! You'll make a tempting serving wench at the costume ball."

"I can't believe I'm going to an actual costume ball," I said, my stomach fluttering with excitement. From the moment Craig and I had moved into the neighborhood, we'd been pulled into one whirlwind fund-raiser after another, and we loved it. The costume ball was yet another fund-raiser. This year, the proceeds were going to the public schools for computer equipment.

"I showed you my costume, now you show me yours." There would be costume judging at the ball, and to keep the judging fair—since the judges were local—everyone at the ball was required to wear a mask with their costumes.

The winner of the "best costume award" received dinner for two at the restaurant of their choice, and a trophy. Since the entire neighborhood consisted of middle-to-upper class working families, the dinner wasn't the lure; it was the coveted trophy.

According to Isabelle, Kyle Bradford, who lived in the biggest, nicest house on the block, had won the trophy for three years running.

"I'm sick of him gloating, Kristen," Isabelle said. "I don't care who wins, as long as it's not Kyle." She opened a box on the bed beside her and held up a leopard-skin, one-piece jumpsuit. "I'm going as a cat woman this year."

Isabelle was a pretty woman with curly, shoulder-length hair and light blue eyes. She and Craig were trying to have their first baby, but after six months with no results, I knew Isabelle was beginning to grow anxious.

Craig and I had decided to wait another two years to have our first child. Right now, we were enjoying our freedom and just being together. We had spent the entire weekend decorating the outside of the house for Halloween, complete with a ghost in the trees and a witch on the house.

"You'll look wonderful in that costume," I said, not bothering to hide my envy. It was true. Isabelle was as sleek and slender as a reed, while I had to watch every calorie and jog three times a week just to stay a size ten. "So, do you know what Matthew is going to be?"

With a snort, Isabelle shook her head. "He'll probably go as Dracula. He does every year."

"Craig is going as a Viking warrior," I said.

"That's a good choice. I wished that Matthew would be something different for a change."

I glanced at my watch. "I just hope Craig makes it to the costume store before they close. He always waits until the last minute for everything. Sometimes it drives me crazy." I gave Isabelle a wan smile. "Makes me wonder how on earth he can be such a good lawyer, as absentminded as he is!"

Isabelle nodded with complete sympathy. "I sometimes wonder the same thing about Matthew."

Both of our husbands practiced law, but with different firms. Craig practiced criminal law, and Matthew was a corporate lawyer, so they never lacked for conversation and seemed to thrive on getting into heated debates.

The ringing of the phone interrupted our conversation. I picked up the extension in our bedroom. "Hello?"

"Honey?"

I covered the mouthpiece and whispered to Isabelle, "It's Craig. Bet you a dollar he's going to be late." I settled the phone against my ear again. "Hi, babe."

"I'm running a little late here, Kristen."

I mouthed the words, "I told you so" to Isabelle, who grinned and shook her head as if she'd heard it all before.

"How late? The ball starts at nine o'clock."

"You'd better start without me," my husband said.

"I don't want to go without you," I said, trying not to whine. It was my first ball, and I was nervous enough without Craig!

"I'll go with you," Isabelle said. "I'll leave a note for Matthew and ask him to wait for Craig, then they can come together later."

Relief flooded my knees. As long as I didn't have to walk in alone, I didn't care. "Did you hear Isabelle, Craig? She's going to go with me, and have Matthew wait for you."

"Super. See you there, hon."

"Bye."

I stifled an irritated sigh as I hung up. "Looks like it will be the cat woman and the serving wench for a while."

"It wouldn't be the first time for me," Isabelle said. "Last year, Matthew got tied up and didn't make it until they were announcing the best costume."

88

The ball was held at the neighborhood community center. Isabelle had told me that the house had been donated by an eccentric neighbor who had died of cancer. After his death, everyone had chipped in for the remodeling, leaving the entire bottom floor capable of holding three hundred people for various events and parties. There was also a fishing lake, and small golf course, paid for by the homeowners in the area.

Craig and I had willingly paid our dues when we'd purchased our house.

By the time Isabelle and I arrived, the building was packed with a crazy array of costumes. I watched in amazement as a huge pumpkin made a clumsy attempt to dance with a wicked witch. There was Frankenstein, a fairy, and more than one devil and several angels. I was relieved when I didn't see a Viking warrior in sight, which meant that Craig would be the only Viking at the party.

Perhaps he'll have a chance at winning the trophy, I thought as Isabelle and I made our way to the refreshment table. The long table groaned beneath dozens of freakish hors d'oeuvre. Among them were eyeballs and fingers and liver pate de foie gras in the shape of a brain.

Isabelle handed me a cup of blood-red punch. I peered at the liquid with understandable suspicion.

"The strips of bloody meat are mashed strawberries," Isabelle volunteered with a smile. "And the white bones are coconut flakes."

I took a sip, surprised to find it delicious. But I detected the alcohol right away. I hated to admit it, but I was a lousy drinker.

"Yes, Kristen, it's spiked," Isabelle said, laughing. "Go ahead, enjoy yourself!"

I guess it was pride that kept me from telling her about my lack of tolerance for alcohol. Feeling reckless, I drank the punch and accepted another from a passing zombie carrying a tray. Looking around, I saw several more zombies, all carrying trays filled with gruesome hors d'oeuvres, or bloody punch. It was a nice touch, or should I say—a horrifying touch? I smiled, feeling a slight buzz from the punch.

Even without Craig, I was having fun. The realization surprised me.

A ghoulish-looking man with a bloody knife sticking from his head practically fell into Isabelle. He grabbed her arm. "Let's dance, pussycat."

Laughing, Isabelle tried to push him away. I could tell that he was drunk.

"I'm married, ghoul. Go rob a grave or something."

"C'mon, let's dance!" he persisted, yanking on Isabelle's long tail. With a squeal, she was pulled into the crowd of dancers.

Grinning, I watched her dance with the ghoul. It was obvious she was having a high old time, too. I glanced at my watch and saw that we'd been at the party nearly an hour.

"More blood, Madam?"

I turned to find a zombie holding out his tray. With a reckless shrug, I snatched another cup of punch, plopping my empty glass on the tray. Before he could disappear, I reached out and snagged a second drink. Isabelle would be thirsty after her dance, I reasoned.

But Isabelle went from a ghoul to a mummy, and then to a scary-looking werewolf who tried to sling her over his shoulder.

So I drank my punch and hers. By this time the room had began to move a little, only I knew that it wasn't really the room, but my head. I was pleasantly plastered, I realized, smiling at everyone and anything.

Frankenstein bumped into me. He reached out to steady me, and I felt his hand dip into my cleavage. Before I could voice my outrage, he howled with laughter and pointed to my chest.

There was a bloody hand sticking out of my bodice, unattached. Not his hand, of course. I could see that now. I pulled the hand free and threw it at him, laughing. Just a little clean, harmless fun, I told myself.

I finally spotted a Viking warrior across the crowded room. "Craig!" I shouted in my excitement, jumping up and waving.

The Viking ignored me in favor of an angel. They began dancing. I suffered a flash of jealousy, but quickly quelled it. It was a party; we were allowed to dance with other people. Craig had probably been looking for me when he got snagged by a passing angel.

I giggled at the thought, and my giggles turned into hiccups. It was hard to focus on the Viking across the room, but I tried. I had no idea where Isabelle had gone.

When arms slipped around me from behind, my first thought was that Craig had managed to get through the crowd. I looked over my shoulder and nearly shrieked as Dracula showed me his impressive fangs in a grin.

Not Craig, but Matthew as Dracula, I figured, relieved that it was someone I knew. The entire time I'd been there, I hadn't recognized anyone. The costumes were that concealing.

"Oh, it's you," I said, trying to pull free of his arms. I wasn't so drunk that I didn't realize Matthew was being a little too friendly with his hands. They kept creeping up to cover my breasts, and I had to push them down.

It fast became obvious that Matthew was so smashed that he didn't realize what he was doing. He'd never made a pass at me before. It horrified me to think of Isabelle seeing him make one now and thinking I was reciprocating.

Still struggling against his amazingly strong hold, I spotted the coatroom to our left. I changed my strategy and leaned into him as if I wanted to dance. He made a satisfied noise in his throat and pulled me close.

I steadily steered him to the coat check, praying Craig and Isabelle weren't watching. Dracula's hands hugged my buttocks in a most embarrassing way. I couldn't wait to get him alone so that I could talk some sense into him, berate him for his outrageous actions, remind him that his wife was my best friend, and that my husband was his best friend.

Finally, I could reach out and grasp the doorknob. I opened the door and let myself fall backward, toward the closet. Obviously, I'd caught him off-balance, for the momentum propelled us deep into the closet. I tried to catch myself, but only succeeded in pulling a rack of coats along with me.

I landed on my back, and Dracula landed on top of me. Now we were hopelessly buried in coats, both of us too drunk to maneuver with any sort of dignity. I couldn't help it, I began to laugh, and once I began, I couldn't seem to stop. The entire situation struck me as hilarious funny.

Maybe if I hadn't been laughing so hard and helplessly, I would have realized Matthew's intent before it was too late. Maybe I would have realized that he wasn't attempting to untangle us from the heavy coats, but trying to get my underwear off!

At least, this was the excuse I used later during one of my many horrifying reflections back to this night when I asked myself the well-worn question: How did this happen?

It was over in a matter of moments, and in another moment, Matthew was gone, leaving me a lot more sober and stunned into a paralyzing shock.

I lay there, suffocating beneath the mass of coats, my voluptuously sexy skirt squashed against my chest and my thighs bare. Finally, I fought the coats from me and stumbled to my feet, pushing my skirt down and adjusting my mask. It was dark in the closet, so I had no idea where my panties were. At the moment, my underwear was the least of my worries!

What would I do? What would I say? My head was spinning and had begun to throb. Oh, why did I drink that second and third glass of punch? I knew that I couldn't handle liquor!

This was worse than horrible—it was devastating! I'd had sex with my best friend's husband. And I had cheated on my husband with his best friend! Never mind that I wasn't participating—I hadn't fought him, either! And I didn't think Craig nor Isabelle would believe my preposterous story of laughing so hard I didn't realize what

Matthew was doing! Even to my own ears, the explanation sounded ludicrous.

I put my hands to my scalded cheeks, struggling with disbelief. Maybe it was a nightmare. I jumped at the possibility, but I had barely managed to grasp it when the closet door came open.

"Kristen! There you are!" Isabelle shouted cheerfully. "Someone said they spotted you going into the closet."

My heart thrashed against my rib cage. Oh, God! Had someone told Isabelle that Dracula had been with me? Did she know?

"What's wrong?" Isabelle came further into the closet, frowning now. "You look pale, and I don't think it's the makeup. Are you sick?"

It was the opening I needed, so I pounced. "Yes, yes. I have a horrible headache—a migraine, I think. I'm going to go home." I stepped past Isabelle and into the light of the party, shielding my eyes. I didn't want to face anyone. "Tell—tell Craig that I left, would you?" I have to get home and take a shower, I thought, clinging to that single thread of sanity.

"I'll go with you," Isabelle announced. "You'll need someone to drive you if you have a migraine. Lord knows I know how one of those feel."

Before I could protest, Isabelle took my arm and led me to the door. "They'll realize we left, Kristen. Let's get you home and into bed."

Guilt swamped me. Isabelle was a wonderful friend, and I had betrayed her! With a muffled moan, I allowed her to lead me down the walk to her car.

By the time we arrived at my house, my fabricated migraine had become a reality. The moment I cleared the threshold, I headed for the bathroom. Isabelle stood over me as I filled the toilet with blood-red punch, then placed a cold washcloth to my forehead before leading me to bed.

"Here, take these." She handed me some aspirin and a cup of water. I swallowed them obediently, unable to look at her without remembering what had happened.

"I'm okay now," I choked out, trying not to cry. I didn't want to arouse Isabelle's suspicions.

"Well, I'll stay for a while," Isabelle said reluctantly. "Then if I see that you're sleeping, I'll go back to the party and let Craig know."

Craig! Oh, God, how can I tell Craig? How can I expect him to understand, or love me afterward? I slept with another man! I had committed adultery!

Maybe I wouldn't tell him.

The thought came out of nowhere, and wouldn't go away.

What if I forgot it ever happened? What if I pretended it never happened?

But then, what if Matthew told someone?

My head continued to throb as I tried to figure out what to do. Finally, I must have dozed off, for the next thing I knew, Craig was crawling into bed beside me.

I lay there, very still, praying he'd believe that I was still sleeping. When I heard him snoring, I let out a slow, shaky breath of relief. Thank God, I wouldn't have to face him just yet. . . .

The next morning, I overslept. Craig was gone when I awoke, much to my relief. I worked part-time as a receptionist for a prestigious pediatrician, so I didn't have to go to work. I wasn't sure that I could have, anyway.

I fixed myself a cup of coffee and sat at the kitchen table, still undecided over what to do. Should I just forget about it? What if Matthew didn't even remember? As I recalled, he had seemed fairly drunk, so wasn't it possible that he wouldn't remember?

Finally, I came to the conclusion that I would try to forget about the incident. I just couldn't see a reason to speak up and hurt the people I loved most.

That evening when Craig came home from work, he slipped up behind me and whispered in my ear, "I had a fantastic time last night. How about you?"

My mouth went bone-dry. I slowly laid down the knife I'd been using to slice mushrooms for a salad, afraid I'd cut myself. "Sure," I said. "I had a good time, too."

And I had been having a good time, until Dracula came along! I knew that I'd never be able to watch another movie about vampires without being reminded of the costume ball.

Craig nuzzled my neck. "Have we got time for a quickie before Matthew and Isabelle get here?"

I froze. "Matthew and Isabelle are coming over?"

Craig chuckled. "Of course, silly! We've had this date planned for a few weeks now. It's their anniversary, and they wanted to celebrate it with us. You offered to make dinner for them, remember?"

I had forgotten! Oh, God, I'd have to face them—all three of them! My stomach churned. Could I do it? My palms grew damp. Could I pull it off? Could I look at Matthew and pretend he'd never made love to me in that coat closet?

For everyone's sake, I knew that I had to.

"Of course, I remember," I said, forcing a laugh. "And no, we don't have time for a quickie. You do have time to take out the trash and get in the shower, though."

Once he was gone, I rushed to the freezer and took out two more steaks, throwing them into the microwave to thaw. I added more lettuce to the salad, and put a bottle of wine in the freezer to chill.

By the time Craig came into the kitchen after his shower, I had composed myself. "Would you mind starting the grill on the patio, hon?"

I realized my mistake the moment he'd gone to do my bidding. The doorbell rang, leaving me to answer it! Taking a deep breath, I removed my apron and walked on shaky legs to the front door. I pasted a smile on my face and opened it.

Isabelle kissed me on the cheek, and brushed by at the speed of light. Matthew stared at me, lifting one brow in a questioning way. "You look a little flushed, Kristen. We didn't interrupt anything, did we?"

My face flooded with color as his meaning sank in. "No, you didn't. Come in."

There had been no recognition in his eyes, I realized, my legs nearly buckling with relief. So he was either pretending it never happened, or he didn't remember it happening.

Either way was fine by me!

At the end of the meal, Isabelle and Craig volunteered to serve coffee and desert, leaving me alone at the table with Matthew. I waited, inwardly trembling. Surely if he was going to mention the closet interlude, he would do it now. I was so tense with expectation that I literally jumped when he finally spoke.

"So, Kristen, aside from your hellish migraine, did you enjoy the ball last night?"

I licked my lips, studying my glass of water. Did his question hold a double meaning? I couldn't tell. "I, um, was having a good time . . . until the migraine." Oh, God, what if he thought I meant that I actually enjoyed his clumsy actions?

"Good. I always have a fantastic time, but I think last night was the best."

I swallowed hard and kept my gaze lowered, waiting for him to continue. I could hear the blood rushing through my veins, fired by a jolt of adrenaline.

"It's a pity you didn't get to stay for the costume award—"

"Kristen, where's the sugar bowl? I can't find it."

It was Isabelle calling from the kitchen. I leaped to my feet and rushed from the dining room as if I were on fire.

I'd heard all I wanted to hear from Matthew.

But what I heard in the kitchen was almost as bad.

The moment Craig left carrying the cheesecake, saucers, and forks, Isabelle grabbed my arm and pulled me close, her eyes gleaming with the joy of sharing gossip.

"Guess what Marta and Elena found when they cleaned up after the party today?"

I hadn't a clue. "I give up. What did they find?"

"Someone's panties in the coat closet!" Isabelle giggled. "I would give up my credit card at the most posh store at the mall to discover to whom they belonged! They were red satin, the slinky kind with the thong and a pattern of embroidered hearts across the front."

I managed a weak smile and secretly thanked God they weren't monogrammed, because Isabelle had just described my panties. As it was, they were unusual enough to cause a fuss! Oh, why oh why hadn't I just slipped on a pair of old-fashioned cotton panties beneath my costume?

"Say, you didn't see anyone in there when you were looking for your coat, did you?"

"Looking for my—oh, yeah. Um, no, I didn't."

"Well, too bad. Obviously someone had a quickie in the closet."

I gripped the counter, holding onto my weak smile for all it was worth. "Yeah, I guess they did."

"We're thinking about holding a meeting and auctioning them off," Isabelle said, chuckling as if she were already envisioning the look on the owner's face.

My stomach bottomed out. I was deathly afraid that I was going to be sick right then and there. For the life of me, I didn't know how I managed to laugh right along with her. If my laughter sounded forced, Isabelle didn't seem to notice.

"Are they really going to do that?" I croaked out, inwardly horrified at the thought. I wasn't certain, of course, but there was a possibility that Craig could identify my underwear. He knew about my underwear fetish, and he had seen me dress that very morning. Would he remember? It was a chance I wasn't willing to take.

"I don't know. They're still thinking about it."

"Who—who has them?" I bit my lip, hoping Isabelle wouldn't wonder about the question. I had tried to sound casual.

"Marta has them in her car, under the driver's seat. I think she's planning on playing a joke on her husband, get him back for the time he had those roses delivered and claimed he didn't send them. For two days he nearly drove her bonkers demanding she tell him her lover's name." Isabelle laughed as she added, "I think he nearly convinced her that she did have a lover."

I made it through the rest of the night without losing my mind, although I came close a few more times. After Isabelle and Matthew left, Craig and I watched a movie, then went to bed.

When I was certain he was sound asleep, I sneaked out of bed, grabbing the clothes I'd deliberately left out as I left the bedroom and carefully closed the door behind me.

I'd chosen a black turtleneck, dark jeans, and a baseball cap. I also wore a puffy ski jacket. When I had dressed, I paused to look in the hall mirror, gasping at how huge my eyes seemed, and how pale my face looked. I looked like a thief, and I hoped that I was about to become a successful one.

I slipped out the back door to the alley, moving from shadow to shadow and praying that no one would see me. If I got caught taking the panties out of Marta's car, everyone would know about my dirty little secret.

Two blocks later, I came to Marta's backyard. I eyed the privacy fence with dismay. Finally, with a determined chin, I awkwardly scaled the fence, picking up several splinters in my hands.

I ignored the sting of the splinters, nearly breaking my ankle when I dropped to the other side into Marta's backyard. So far, so good. No dogs had been alerted to my presence.

Moving stealthily, I made my way to the door leading into the garage from the backyard. Thankfully, it was unlocked, or my mission would have failed right then and there.

The garage smelled of gasoline and motor oil. My sneakers crunched on oil dry, spread on the garage floor to absorb fluid leaks. I froze and listened.

Nothing but silence, broken by the occasional, distant sound of a dog barking. It was dark and cold in the garage. I shivered as I felt my way to Marta's car, then began searching for the door handle.

The passenger door was locked.

Frustrated, I circled the car, keeping my hands on the vehicle for guidance. The driver's side was unlocked!

When I opened it, the dome light came on, of course, nearly blinding me and scaring the living daylights out of me. I quickly knelt and stuck my hand beneath the seat, searching for the touch of silk.

I found them! With a silent whoop of joy, I backed out of the car with my panties and closed the door gently, then leaned against it, breathing hard and fast.

Finally, after muttering a quick prayer of thanks, I stuffed my panties in my pocket and reversed my path. This time when I scaled the privacy fence, I did a better job—boosted, perhaps, by my successful panty raid.

I didn't relax until I was once again in my own house.

In the darkened kitchen, I leaned against the counter, clutching my panties and wondering what I should do with them. I didn't want to keep them, didn't ever want to see them again. They were a painful reminder of something I would rather forget.

In the end, I stuffed them inside an empty coffee can and buried the can in the kitchen trash. Then and only then was I able to return to my bed and sleep.

The evidence had been confiscated. Now there was no way anyone could find out about my illicit meeting in the coat closet with my next-door neighbor—unless my next-door neighbor spilled the beans.

I didn't think that he would; I had to believe that he wouldn't.

For a few days, there was a grumbling buzz amongst the women in the neighborhood over the missing panties. Their fun was over, and now they would never know who had done what in the coat closet at the community house.

The matter was finally dropped altogether, and I was able to breathe easier.

Over the next few weeks, I became quite good at forgetting my encounter with "Dracula," as I preferred to think of him. Only at odd times of the day did I remember, and then I managed to put it from my mind fairly quickly.

Matthew never hinted about it again, and Craig and Isabelle appeared to suspect nothing.

It was as if it never happened.

I might eventually have been able to convince myself of this had life continued as it was.

But, of course, this was not to be.

The day I lost my morning coffee in the toilet, I was hit by a startling realization.

I was two weeks late on my period.

The blood drained from my face as I crumpled to the bathroom floor. Nausea, late on my period . . . it wasn't difficult to figure out that there was a good chance that I was pregnant.

Since Craig and I knew we would eventually have children, the news should have been joyous.

But it wasn't, because I remembered how it must have happened.

Craig and I always used protection.

The night of the ball, Matthew hadn't.

Or at least I didn't think that he had, considering the brevity of the act and his hasty departure.

I was going to have Dracula's baby.

Moaning, I closed my eyes. I hadn't thought it could get worse, but obviously, I'd been wrong.

Keeping an unwitting act of adultery from my husband was one thing, but having another man's baby was quite another.

I was left with no choice but to tell him. My marriage would be over. I would lose everything.

Depressed, frightened, and heartsick, I went to bed and stayed there, claiming I had the flu.

Craig was his usual, attentive self, bringing me soup and checking on me several times a day. His thoughtfulness only succeeded in increasing my guilt.

"I think you should see a doctor," he told me on the third day as he came home from work and immediately began fussing over me.

Listlessly, I shook my head. "It's just the flu. I'll be better soon. I just need to rest."

When Craig wasn't hovering over me, Isabelle was bringing me juice and magazines, sitting in a chair by the door so that she could chat with me. I didn't know which was worse, having to face Isabelle or Craig.

"I thought I was pregnant this month," Isabelle announced on the fourth day of my "sickness." She was flipping through a magazine, one of the many she'd brought me, looking for a recipe she'd forgotten to clip.

She sounded so disappointed I wanted to cry. I was having her husband's baby, yet she was the one that wanted it! It was so bizarre I could scarcely believe it myself. Oh, how she'll hate me! I thought, cringing as I imagined her horrified face.

"Did you hear me, Kristen?"

I stared at the ceiling, battling tears of self-pity for me and sympathy for Isabelle. "Yes, I heard you. I'm sorry. Maybe next month you'll get lucky."

Isabelle sighed. "I don't know why it's taking so long. The doctors say both of us are fine, and it can't be for lack of trying. Matthew and I make love almost every night."

Girl talk. I swallowed hard, inwardly whimpering. Little did Isabelle know that I was not deserving of her confidence. I wasn't deserving of her friendship at all. I was lower than pond scum, and keeping my secret inside was slowly driving me insane.

"I want a baby so badly, and I know that Matthew feels the same way."

I'd bet he wouldn't feel that way if he knew that I was having his first child! The conversation, combined with the chicken noodle soup Isabelle had fixed for my lunch, was more than I could stand.

On shaky legs, I ran to the bathroom and threw up.

I saw Isabelle's shadow on the commode lid as she came up behind me.

"Are you sure you're not pregnant, Kristen?"

I hid my flushed face in my arms, ignoring her question and praying she would go away before my hysteria forced me to scream out my terrible secret.

But I couldn't tell Isabelle without telling Craig first, and I hadn't worked up the nerve for that yet.

"Because this flu seems to be lasting a long time. You should at least go to the doctor."

She brushed a hand against my hair, her voice so full of friendly sympathy I wanted to crawl inside the commode and flush myself down into the sewer where I belonged.

"I can drive you. I'll even go in with you, if you're scared."

My voice was hoarse from retching as I said, "No thanks, Isabelle. I'm sure I'll be fine in a couple of days." I would be fine when hell froze over, I added to myself.

"Why don't you go on home? I—I think I'll take a nap. Craig will be home soon, so he can take over nursing."

I didn't want anyone to nurse me, but I'd quickly discovered my protests were falling on deaf ears.

"I'll leave when you get back into bed and prove to me that you're going to sleep."

Isabelle could be a steamroller when she put her mind to it, I discovered. Knowing it was useless to fight, I let her help me to bed, fluff my pillows, and tuck me in. I half expected her to read me a story.

When she finally left, I closed my eyes.

The next time I opened them, Craig was standing above me. His expression held a mixture of fear and excitement. He was holding a small white bag.

"Isabelle hinted that you might need one of these," he said, leaning down to place a lingering kiss on my mouth.

I frowned at the sack, wondering what Isabelle had said to him. "What is it?"

"A pregnancy test." At my horrified look, Craig sat on the bed and took me into his arms. "Oh, honey, did you think I would be disappointed? I won't—I'm not. I know it's sooner than we'd planned, but it's fine with me if you're ready. I mean, I'm ready if you are!"

Tears flowed from my eyes as if I had sprung a leak. I couldn't control them. I began to sob in earnest. Craig crooned and held me as if I were a baby until my sobs subsided. Finally, he pulled back to look into my eyes.

"Will you take this test so we can celebrate?"

I wiped at my eyes and drew in a shaky breath. "I'll take the test."

I would have to tell him soon. I would have to tell my husband that yes, I was pregnant, but no, he wasn't the father.

And then I would have to tell him my horrible, unbelievable story!

How could anyone believe such a ridiculous tale? What if he went into a rage and tried to kill Matthew? What if he flew into a rage and tried to kill me? I'd never seen Craig react violently, but I knew that everyone was capable of violence, some more than others were.

Trembling with dread, I sent Craig into the kitchen to start supper. When he'd gone, I took the test and locked myself in the bathroom.

Why am I dreading it? I asked myself. I knew that it would be positive. I was a smart, educated woman. I knew the symptoms, and I had more than my share to convince me.

Poor Isabelle! She wanted so badly to have a baby, yet I was the lucky one—or so she would believe.

Would Craig insist we tell Isabelle and Matthew? My skin grew clammy at the thought. A cold sweat trickled down my spine. I leaned against the bathroom door and closed my eyes against the conjured images. Terrible images. Unimaginable images.

My best friend would be devastated, as well as hurt and angry. I dreaded Isabelle's reaction almost as much as I dreaded telling Craig.

In a perfect world, Craig would forgive me, insist we tell no one, and move away from this neighborhood and all its reminders. In a perfect world, Craig would insist we think of the baby as his. Ours. He would not stop loving me, or blame me for what happened.

But it wasn't a perfect world, and I knew I had to face the facts.

Most likely Craig would want a divorce. The sight of me would disgust him—sicken him.

The sound of Craig's voice through the door that was against my ear startled me. I stifled a shriek.

"If you don't come out of there in two minutes, I'm coming in after you."

I opened the door, thrust out a determined chin, and said in a shaky voice, "I need to talk to you, Craig."

He grinned, his eyes bright with anticipation. "Is it positive? Are we going to have a baby?"

I felt so badly, I wanted to die right there on the spot. "Come into the kitchen. I need to tell you something."

Craig's grin faltered at my tortured tone. He followed me silently to the kitchen table and took a seat. I fidgeted with the chair, but didn't immediately sit down.

By this time, Craig was anxious about what I had to say, no doubt alarmed by my gloomy face. "What is it, Kristen?"

I clutched the chair until my knuckles whitened, staring anywhere but at Craig as I began to tell my story about Dracula and the coat closet.

He didn't interrupt, but I had no idea what he was thinking or feeling, because I simply felt too ashamed to look at him. Once, I thought he made a smothered sound, but I never faltered with my story. I told him everything. I even told him about my panty raid.

"I swear to you, Craig, that everything I've just told you is the God's honest truth. I didn't realize what was happening until it was too late, or I would never have let it happen." My voice shook badly. Tears ran down my face and fell onto my hands. "It all happened so fast. . . ."

A snorting sound came from Craig's direction. I risked a peek, wincing when I saw that he'd covered his face with his hands. Oh, God, he was crying!

But then Craig dropped his hands and I saw that I was wrong. He wasn't crying, he was laughing!

"But—I—I don't understand!" I cried. "How can you find this funny?"

He was laughing hard now, his face red with the effort, mirthful tears rolling down his cheeks, his hands clutching his knees. He took a great breath and nearly tipped his chair over as he launched into another round of laughter.

I just stood there in shock and disbelief as Craig continued to laugh uproariously.

"My God, Craig!" I finally shouted, growing angry. "How can you laugh about this?"

"Be—because!" Craig tried to say, but lapsed into laughter again. After a moment, he tried again. "Because I was Dracula! I was the man in the coat closet. I was the man who made love to you, Kristen!"

I nearly fainted. "W-what?"

"Yes, it was me! At the last minute, Matthew and I decided to switch costumes to see how long it would take you gals to realize what we'd done. When you pulled me into the coat closet, I thought that you'd recognized me."

The room began to whirl in a sickening way. I pulled out the chair and fell into it, dazed.

"When I saw you in that outfit, with your breasts spilling out all over the place, I was so turned on, I just went crazy. I had to have you, right then and there on the floor."

It was Craig all along? My brain was slow to realize what my ears were hearing. All this time I had been agonizing over this, and it had been Craig all along?

I stared at Craig, who had once again succumbed to a bout of belly-rolling laughter. When he slid from his chair and collapsed on the floor, still laughing, I kicked him.

I was furious, and I didn't know why. I think it was a delayed reaction. For the past month or so, I had been going through hell, the guilt nearly killing me.

And Craig thought it was funny?

Well—I didn't.

He grabbed my foot when I tried to kick him a second time, and pulled me out of the chair and onto the floor with him, laughing at my struggles.

"Baby, don't be mad," he coaxed, chuckling. "If I'd had any idea that you'd been torturing yourself this long, I would have said something! I thought that you knew! I said something about having a great time, and you said that you had, too."

Slowly, I was beginning to see why Craig had believed that I had known he was Dracula. It all began to make sense.

The rest hit me like a ton of bricks.

I was pregnant, and it was my husband's baby. I hadn't committed adultery. I hadn't betrayed Isabelle.

All was well and right again in my world.

A giggle rumbled through my chest. Then another, and another, until together, Craig and I were laughing so hard we didn't hear the doorbell ring. It wasn't until Isabelle whistled that we realized we were no longer alone.

We stared at our friends standing in the doorway, watching us as if we'd lost our mind.

"Well," Isabelle demanded. "Are we going to have a baby, or not?"

I shot Craig a mock glare. "Don't you dare," I warned.

His eyes lit with mirth. His lips twitched. He opened his mouth, and I quickly clamped my hand over it.

"Yes," I told the waiting couple. "We're going to have a baby."

The moment I let my hand drop, Craig rolled from me and leaped to his feet. He grabbed Matthew by the arm and pulled him out of the room. "Man, have I got a story for you!"

Bemused, Isabelle watched them disappear. Then she turned to look at me. "What's going on? I feel like I'm missing something."

With a groan, I scrambled to my feet. I held out my hand, indicating she sit down. "I might as well tell you."

"Tell me what?"

"That I thought I was going to have Dracula's baby." I kept a straight face with an effort. Isabelle stared at me, uncomprehending.

"By Dracula, you mean Craig, right?"

"Well, I didn't know that until now."

"I think you'd better start at the beginning," Isabelle said, beginning to look concerned about my sanity.

So, I told my friend the whole, ridiculous story.

THE END

PHANTOM LOVER
He Helped Me Move On.

"**A**re you all right, Angie?"

Rosemary stood in the doorway, looking at me with concern in her eyes.

"I'm fine," I said, attempting a smile. "Why?"

"You don't seem like yourself today and besides that, you look a little washed out."

"It's just a bit of a headache," I said with a shrug. "No big deal."

"We're slow today. Do you want me to finish that up so you can go home?" she asked, indicating the tomatoes I was busily slicing for the salad buffet.

"Don't be silly. I told you I'm fine."

She gave me a skeptical look, then grabbed a plate of butter pats from the cooler and left the kitchen. When she disappeared through the swinging double doors, I ran a cloth under the faucet and pressed it against my forehead.

The fact was I'd been feeling a little off all day and I probably should've taken Rosemary up on her offer. I'd worked at the bistro ever since graduating from high school six years before. What started out as merely a summer job had developed into a career, and I knew that Rosemary considered me one of her most valued employees. Heck, she probably would've paid me for a full day, regardless of whether I stayed or not, so it wasn't the fear of losing a half day's pay that made me stick it out. No, if it had been any day but October thirty-first I would have been out the door in a heartbeat.

You see, Halloween is my favorite day of the year. I was invited to a fabulous costume party and I told myself that there was no way I was going to be sick and miss out on the fun.

Ten minutes later, with my tomatoes sliced paper-thin and my radishes sculpted into tiny rosebuds, I went out front to restock the buffet. Glancing around, I saw that Rosemary was right. The bistro was unusually quiet, with only three of our eleven booths occupied. Even so, I struggled through the rest of my shift, all the while trying to convince myself that I felt okay.

It was unseasonably warm for late October, but after the heat of the kitchen, the air outside the bistro was a welcome relief. I glanced past Coleman Street, where the autumn foliage that decorated the hillside was still magnificent. West Lawrence is not a pretty town, and the kaleidoscope of fall colors softened the ugliness of the factories and the weather-beaten storefronts.

When I got home the house was dark and silent. My mother was visiting my aunt, Sheila, in Seattle. My brother was still at work and my older sister, Nancy, had moved out years before. I don't usually like to be alone, but that day the quiet was a welcome change. I decided to lie down for a while, since I had a couple of hours before I had to get ready for the costume party, and see if I could ditch the screaming headache that was torturing me all day. I'd just sprawled out across my bed when my cell phone rang. Each of my friends has a different ring tone, and when I heard the Red Hot Chili Peppers, I knew it was my best friend, Ruth, calling.

"What's up, Ruthie?" I asked, flipping the phone open.

"Are we still going tonight?"

"Of course."

"Okay. The thing is, my brother's car broke down, so I have to pick up his goofy girlfriend at the airport. I'm leaving now, but I'm going to be late for the party. Want to just meet me there?"

I sighed. "I guess."

She hesitated. "I found out today that Bobby is definitely going to be there. He specifically asked if you were going."

"Then I'm not going."

"Of course you're going, Angie! And Bobby is probably going to want to ask you out and I hope you'll say yes for once. He's a great guy and he's crazy about you. I wish you'd give him a chance."

"I'm hanging up now, Ruthie. I'll see you at the party."

I flipped my phone shut, set my alarm for six o'clock, and lay back against my pillows. Drifting off to sleep, I found myself thinking about Bobby, the computer guru who'd recently repaired my laptop. He's cute beyond belief. There's nothing wrong with Bobby at all, but there was definitely something wrong with me. My thoughts flickered briefly to Perry. How can I go on living when Perry is gone? I felt the stab of pain that hadn't lessened one bit in the five years since Perry's death, and then I felt the guilt that's never far behind. But neither of those feelings is going to bring him back, and they weren't going to help my headache, either, so I pushed them away and drifted off to sleep.

I woke up fifteen minutes before the alarm went off, feeling only slightly better. I rolled my head carefully from side to side. My headache was still there, but now it was reduced to a dull pounding. After a long, hot shower I dried my hair, put on some makeup, and went to the closet to retrieve my costume. I looked at it and smiled. It was a different version of the costume I'd worn every year since I was five: a princess dress and cape.

When I was little my mom did the best she could, fashioning costumes out of my grandma's old cocktail dresses and bed sheets dyed in shades of lavender and pink. My father disappeared when I was two, leaving Mom struggling to pay the bills. I longed for nice things and on that first Halloween I felt just like Cinderella after a visit from her Fairy Godmother. After that, I always dressed as a princess on Halloween, maybe subconsciously trying to recapture that special childhood memory.

I smiled again as I ran my hands over the gown's silky, blue fabric and the tiny sequins sprinkled across the bodice. I bought it at a costume shop in the city and I paid too much for it, but the moment I tried it on I knew the dress was worth every nickel.

Once I slid into the gown and adjusted it to my satisfaction, I slipped on a pair of silver heels and went to work on my hair. I pulled it into a tight ponytail and gelled back the loose strands so they wouldn't show, and then I put on my new wig. When I was satisfied that it looked perfect, I placed a sparkling tiara on my head and finished off the costume with a glittery, black mask that just covered my eyes. I looked in the mirror and smiled. It was perfect.

At seven-thirty I got into my car and headed down the block. Douglas Avenue only has one traffic light, and it always seemed to switch to red the moment I approach. Slamming to a stop, I glanced to my right and my breath caught in my throat.

I always tried to avoid looking at the big, gray house on the corner of Douglas and Bowne, but that night I couldn't keep myself from staring. I've lived in West Lawrence all my life and the house had been abandoned for as long as I could remember. That night the windows glowed with light and music spilled out onto the street. Curious, I craned my neck toward the overgrown shrubbery.

Peering in the windows, I saw people walking around inside the house. The light turned green and I rounded the corner. In front of the house, perched in front of the rusted, wrought-iron gate, a sign said: Spooktacular Halloween Gala. Enter If You Dare!

I nudged the car to the curb and turned off the engine. I sat for a moment, wondering how it was possible that I was seeing what I was seeing. The house looked fantastic. The crumbling, gray siding had been repainted and now looked pearlescent in the light of moon. A riot of red roses climbed up both sides of a trellis and covered the awning in front of the house. How can I have driven by it every day and not notice that someone is making repairs?

Without taking my eyes off the house, I dug my cell phone out of my purse and punched in Ruthie's number. I knew she'd be on her way back from the airport by that time and I wasn't surprised when my call went straight to voice mail.

"Hey, change of plans. It's me who might be late tonight." I briefly described what I saw. "I'm going to go in and see what's going on. I'll catch up with you later."

I flipped my phone shut and I got out of the car, pausing to get myself under control. Luther Lawrence, the millionaire who owned the railroad, built the house in the early 1900s. His mansion was the jewel of the valley in a thriving township until tragedy struck. The village rumor was that Ella Lawrence, Luther's wife, went crazy one night and killed her husband and children in their sleep. Over the years, the rumors of ghost sightings at the house kept most people away, and its increasingly ramshackle condition kept it from being sold. So it sat on the corner of Barclay and Douglas year after year, a painful reminder of better times to a slowly dying town.

To Perry and me, the old house had always been a sanctuary. Walking up the sidewalk, I couldn't help remembering the last time I'd been there—five years previously, a week before Perry died. We didn't use the front door back then. We climbed in through a broken window in the cellar.

Perry and I grew up together. He lived in a big, shabby house on Beverly Street, two blocks over from Douglas. Like everyone else on the north side of town, he came from a big, hardworking family that had a lot more trouble than money. We met in the sandbox at age two and were inseparable ever since. We started kindergarten together, and then middle school, and eventually high school. We suffered through acne and algebra and the absolute pain of living on the edge of poverty. We went from friends to lovers without missing a beat. Having spent our entire lives together, we had no reason to think we wouldn't be together for all of eternity.

There was no privacy in Perry's house or mine, and since neither of us was even close to owning a car, the big, abandoned house was our special place where we went to be alone. It was the place where we drank stolen wine coolers, where we shared our plans and dreams. It was the first place Perry ever kissed me, and the place where he eventually gave me the tiny, heart-shaped diamond I will wear for the rest of my life.

As the memories flooded over me, the pain was ferocious. I wondered what on Earth I was thinking and I abruptly turned to leave.

"Welcome," a deep, masculine voice said.

I turned to see a figure in a cape and mask gliding toward me.

"I hope you're not leaving so soon," he said. "The party's just getting started."

I allowed him to take my elbow and guide me back toward the house. As we stepped beneath the awning, he plucked a rose from the vine and gently tucked it behind my ear, fastening it in place beneath the band of my tiara.

"A rose for a rose," he said with a smile.

I know it sounds silly to say it was love at first sight. I couldn't even see his face behind the mask, but from the moment I saw him I felt a strange surge of tenderness toward the masked man.

Stepping inside, I couldn't quite believe my eyes. Skeleton puppets suspended from wires danced in a corner, their bones clacking, while a pair of remote-control witches stirred up a pot of brew. Spider webs adorned the sparkling chandeliers and bats that looked too real for comfort flitted about the corridors. But underneath the decorations, the house was beautifully clean, with gleaming hardwood floors and polished brass fixtures.

An old record player sat inconspicuously in the corner, playing eerily beautiful music and a long buffet table filled with every kind of food imaginable took up the center of the room. He walked to the buffet table and poured two glasses of punch, handing one of them to me. It was the strangest mixture I'd ever tasted, like every kind of fruit all rolled into one sweet, smooth beverage.

When I finished drinking it, I handed my glass back to the man.

"I didn't even know anyone bought this place. How long have you lived here?"

"I've been here for a long time, Angie," he said softly.

I gaped at him. "How do you know who I am?"

He smiled a sad, mysterious smile, saying nothing.

"That's really not fair. You know me, but I don't have a clue who you are."

"Can't you guess?"

I studied his face, what I could see of it behind the mask. He seemed familiar, but I couldn't quite place him.

"No, I can't. Please tell me."

"Maybe later. For now, may I have the honor of a dance?"

He held out his hands and I was drawn to them. He took me gently into his arms and we swayed to the music, our bodies fitting together as if they were made for each other.

"You're a lovely lady, Angie," he murmured against my hair. "I'll bet you have a lot of boyfriends, don't you?"

"No, not really."

"I can't imagine why."

I pulled back and stared into his face, wondering if my mystery man was Bobby. Deciding it wasn't, I settled back into his embrace.

"I had a boyfriend, but that was a long time ago," I said.

"What happened?" he asked softly.

I never talked about Perry at all, but there was something about the stranger's eyes, something that made him seem like someone I'd known forever. Somehow, it seemed right to tell him.

"We wanted to get married, but we were both from poor families. Jobs around here are scarce and Perry was afraid that he wouldn't be able to support a family, so he joined the military. Our plan was that we would be together, traveling and seeing the world, after he finished his tour."

Memories flashed before my eyes like nightmares, memories of Perry standing tall and proud in his uniform, smiling at me as he said good-bye for the last time. Memories of a phone call in the night, telling me Perry was gone, and me, sinking to the floor, the phone clutched in my hands, unable to stop screaming.

"Perry went to the Middle East," I whispered, tears streaming down my face. "And he never came back."

All at once I felt dizzy. The room swam in and out of focus, and I began to fear that the man had put something in my drink. I don't even know him, for Heaven's sake. What on Earth was I thinking by coming here?

"Are you all right, Angie?"

"I . . . I feel. . . ." But there was no time to think about what I felt. My knees buckled and the room started to go gray. He wrapped me in his arms and held me, and then he whispered a word that went straight through me. It was my name. Not my given name, but the one Perry had called me for as long as I could remember.

"Don't cry for me any more, kitten. Some things just aren't meant to be."

I looked into his eyes, eyes that were as familiar to me as my own. I whispered Perry's name and he gently kissed my lips. And then everything went black.

When I awoke, my head was pounding and Ruthie was shaking me.

"Angie? Are you awake?"

"I think so," I said groggily.

"What in Heaven's name are you doing here?"

"I came for the party, like I told you."

"You didn't tell me anything, and what party?"

I looked around, trying to focus. Everything was gone. There was no buffet, no record player, or dancing skeletons. No witches or chandeliers. The only decorations were dust and the very real cobwebs swaying in the draft that came through the broken windowpanes.

"I don't understand. Where did it all go?" I murmured.

Ruthie rested her hand against my forehead. "Angie, you're burning up."

After practically carrying me out to her car, she sped across town to the ER, where after what seemed an eternally long wait they checked me out and told me I had a nasty case of the flu. They got my fever under control, prescribed rest and plenty of fluids, and sent me on my way.

Back home, Ruthie helped me out of my gown, removed the rose from my hair and set it on the night table, and then tucked me into bed.

"I'm sure glad I sent you that voice mail, or who knows how long I would've laid there on the floor."

"You didn't send me any voice mail, Angie," Ruthie said, fluffing my pillows.

"I certainly did," I insisted. "I called you from the curb before I went inside."

"Well I never got the call." She flipped open her phone and handed it to me. "There's nothing in my inbox. See for yourself."

I scanned the screen. Ruthie's mailbox was empty. "Then how did you know where I was?" I asked, handing the phone back to her.

"I didn't. When you didn't show up at the party I got worried and went looking for you. I saw your car out in front of that old house went inside. Now I'm glad I did."

I hesitated. "Ruthie, you're going to think this is crazy, but there was definitely a party going on there. There was food and music, and there were people. There was this one guy . . . I'm pretty sure it was Perry."

"Sweetie, you were out of head with fever." She turned down my light and gave my hand a squeeze. "Get some rest. I'll see you in the morning."

I fell deeply into sleep and my dreams were filled with memories of Perry. When I awoke the next morning my fever was gone. And so were my feelings of guilt.

Later that afternoon I walked down the street to where my car was still parked in front of the old mansion. Taking a deep breath, I walked through the iron gate and up the walkway. I took a good, long look at the house before me. The siding was gray and crumbling. Some of the porch spindles were missing, while others hung at crazy, broken angles. The rosebush was withered and dead. Tears came to my eyes and I brushed them away with my hands.

"Good-bye, Perry," I whispered.

Everyone thinks I was delirious with fever that night, and I go right on letting them think it. I know in my heart that Perry appeared to me and I don't have to prove that to anyone else. For one magical evening, he returned to me. He reaffirmed our love and gave me permission to go on with my life. Six months have passed, but the rose he gave me sits on my dresser, still as beautiful as ever. For as long as it lives, it will remind me of the night Perry returned from the grave to ease my sorrow.

What we had was the love of a lifetime, and I know that no man will ever take Perry's place in my heart. With Perry's help, I have moved on from the night I got the phone call telling me he was gone, and I know that someday I will be able to find happiness with another man. But for now I have all of my lovely memories of the time I spent with Perry.

And for now, my memories are enough.

THE END

"Do Unto Others" Is The Lesson, Even With—
THE WICKED WITCH NEXT DOOR
When I opened my heart to her, everything changed. .
. .

I looked around at the box-filled living room with a feeling of awe, and then spun around, arms wide, to take it all in. Darren and I had been saving for this for years. This was our dream—owning a house of our own—and at long last, our dream was finally a reality.

Darren came up behind me, wrapped his arms around my waist, and rested his chin on my shoulder. "This is it, babe," he said, his breath warm in my ear. "It's all ours—two bedrooms, a deck in back . . . and a thirty-year mortgage!"

I turned and put my arms around him. Yes, the thirty-year-mortgage part was scary, but this was our home now, and nothing was going to take away from the sheer joy I felt. It'd taken us a long time to reach this point; Darren and I had been married for three wonderful years, but we'd had our share of rough times along the way.

Shortly after our wedding, my father died of a heart attack. I was consoled by the fact that he'd been around long enough to see me get married to Darren, whom he'd liked a lot, but I still missed him every day, and Mom had needed some help for a while as she got used to the idea of living alone for the first time in over thirty years. Then my sister, Kim, announced that she was getting a divorce, and I helped her out by watching her kids in the evenings while she took some business courses at the community college in town.

With all of this going on, Darren and I had postponed the very things we'd wanted most in our own lives—a house and children of our own. We stayed in our cramped little apartment much longer than we'd intended, saving our money for a down payment on a house, laughing at the disastrous meals I concocted using the outdated stove and oven we were forced to make do with. Finally, though, with the help of those extra business courses, Kim was made assistant manager of the beauty salon where she worked, which at least made things a little easier for her and her kids.

And then Darren and I had at last begun house-hunting.

I fell in love with the small, two-bedroom, ranch-style house the first time I saw it. Certainly, it needed some work—the carpets were old and the kitchen cupboards were scratched—but Darren was handy and we knew we'd eventually get it all just exactly the way we wanted it.

I unpacked boxes, arranged our furniture in the rooms a dozen times until they felt just right, and enjoyed the long weekend I'd taken to get these things done. I'd just unpacked the last box on our first Saturday afternoon in our new house when the phone rang. Darren had gone to the hardware store to get some sandpaper, so I rushed to answer it.

"Are you ready for your big housewarming party?" Kim asked.

I groaned. "Give me another month—please. I go back to work on Monday, and right now, all I can think about is when I'm going to find time to paint the bathroom."

"A month? I don't think we can wait that long. In fact, I think we're going to come over . . . right now!"

"What did you say?"

Then the front door burst open and Kim entered, her cell phone at her ear, laughing at my shocked expression. Behind her I saw my mother, my aunts from across town, and a few friends from work. Last to come in, with a sheepish expression on his face, was my husband.

"You knew about this?" I said to Darren, slapping his arm as I pulled the bandana from my head and tried to finger-comb my hair.

He shrugged helplessly. "I couldn't talk them out of it. You know how your mother and your sister get when they make up their minds about something."

Oh, boy, did I know. And I also knew that there was nothing for me to do but make the most of it. So, after freshening up a bit, I went into the kitchen and found that everyone had brought something, so there was plenty of food for all and I had only to relax and enjoy myself. They'd even brought housewarming presents.

It was October and the weather was mild, so Darren got a folding table and some chairs from the garage and set them out on the deck. We moved the party out there, brought out the boom box, and sat around on the folding chairs, talking and laughing.

At dusk, Darren turned on the one light over the back door. "I'll have to install a couple more lights out here," he remarked.

"One thing at a time," I reminded him.

My friends from work had all gone in together and bought Darren and me a new microwave, which we needed badly, and Aunt Clara had knitted us an afghan for our sofa. My mother, knowing I'd been looking forward to having a real kitchen to work in, gave us new cookware, and Kim gave us a set of gourmet cookbooks.

"This is more fun than our wedding shower!" I said, tearing open another box and finding a Crock-Pot from Aunt Agatha.

"Hey, who's that?" Deanna, one of my friends from work, asked suddenly. She pointed toward the yard next to ours.

It was fully dark by then, and I had to strain to see what she was pointing at. In the next yard, which contained a lawn that looked like it hadn't been mowed since midsummer, was an elderly woman. Her long, gray hair fell partway down her back, and we could hear her muttering to herself as she moved around her yard, looking down at the ground as though she'd lost something.

"I don't know; we haven't met any of our neighbors yet," I said uneasily.

"We should invite her over," Darren said, and he started to get up from his folding chair.

"No! Don't!" Kim blurted out.

Darren looked at her in surprise. "Why not?"

In a low voice, Kim said, "She looks like a witch."

Darren rolled his eyes. "Oh, come on," he scoffed.

But I felt my uneasiness growing. The woman was strange, indeed—muttering like that, her dark-colored dress reaching almost to her ankles—and her feet, I saw, covered only by light slippers.

"We can meet her some other time," I said to Darren, putting my hand on his arm.

Always goodhearted, Darren looked like he was going to argue with me about it, but finally, he sat back down and shrugged.

The following Monday I returned to my part-time job working as a bookkeeper for a small insurance company, and I forgot all about the old woman next door. When not at work, I was learning my way around my kitchen, trying out the new Crock-Pot and microwave, and flipping through cookbooks in search of easy recipes to get started on.

Halloween was getting close, so I hung bright, orange, festive fairy lights around our front door, and taped a paper jack-o'-lantern to the window. Then I baked some Halloween cookies, which might've turned out all right if the dough hadn't stuck to my rolling pin.

"Sprinkle a little flour on your countertop and on the rolling pin," my mother suggested when I called her for advice.

"I already tried that," I said, scraping the dough from the rolling pin with a butter knife. "It hasn't worked."

"Then your dough might be too moist."

Later, after supper, Darren bravely bit into one of my cookies. I could hear it crunching as he chewed.

"They're too hard, aren't they?" I wailed. "Mom said my dough was too moist, so I added more flour."

"No, they're fine—really," Darren said, and took another bite.

Crunch, crunch.

I took the plate of cookies out the back door and scraped them into the garbage can. The fact that Darren hadn't even tried to stop me told me that my cookies really were a failure.

I was replacing the lid on the garbage can when I glanced next door—and let out a little squeak of surprise. Our elderly neighbor was in her backyard again. She seemed to have the same old dress and bedroom slippers on, but it'd gotten considerably cooler in the past couple of weeks, and her clothing now seemed downright inadequate. She didn't notice me as she moved slowly around her yard, wringing her hands and muttering. The light over her back porch was on, and I noticed then that her back door hung crooked on its hinge and the window was cracked.

I went back inside and told Darren about what I'd seen.

"So why didn't you go over and introduce yourself?" he asked.

"She gives me the creeps," I said, shivering at the memory of that long, tangled, gray hair. "Maybe she really is a witch."

Darren just shook his head.

Needless to say, I began to watch our neighbor's house more closely, and I noticed that the front of her house didn't look much better than the back. Most of the time the house looked dark and uninhabited, and with the curtains always drawn, it had a closed, unfriendly look about it.

At least I did finally meet some of our other neighbors. Directly across the street from us were Stephanie and her husband, who'd moved into the neighborhood only a year earlier and had two active boys, the oldest in his early teens.

"I haven't met her," Stephanie said when I asked her about our elderly neighbor. "But the boys keep me so busy, there're a lot of people in the neighborhood whom I haven't met yet."

Most of the houses on our street were now decorated with pumpkins and other displays of the season, but even with all of those Halloween decorations up, no house looked as eerie as my neighbor's did, with its dark, unwelcoming windows and broken shutters.

"This is pretty good," Darren said one night, tasting the stroganoff I'd made with our new cookware. He sounded surprised.

"Stephanie gave me the recipe," I told him. "Do you really like it?"

"Yeah, I do," he said, and took a second helping to prove it.

As Halloween drew near, some of the bigger kids in the neighborhood got into the spirit of the season with the occasional prank. The trees in our backyard were toilet-papered, but the mess was minimal and I pulled sheets of Charmin from the branches without much complaint. In fact, I was doing just this when I heard the shouting.

"Yah, witch!"

There was a crash of something metal, and then I looked over to see a couple of preteen boys knocking over my neighbor's garbage can. Moments later, she came hobbling out of her back door, her cane raised high in one hand.

"You boys—stop that this instant!" she called out in a frail, trembling voice.

The boys ran off, but not before calling out, "Witch, witch!" several more times.

I stood frozen in place, my hands full of toilet paper, as the boys ran straight toward me. They hadn't seen me yet in the evening light, and as they came close, I saw that one of them was Stephanie's oldest boy. I reached out and grabbed him by the arm as he went by, the movement so instinctive that I hadn't even thought about doing it.

"Benji, you go home and leave that poor woman alone or I'll tell your mother!" I said, noting with satisfaction his completely shocked expression.

He pulled loose and the boys ran off. But they didn't shout any more, and I knew I'd made an impression. Then I watched as my neighbor stooped with painful slowness to pick up the garbage that was strewn across her backyard. Immediately, my heart went out to her, and I walked across my yard to hers.

"Here—let me help you with that," I said, and bent to pick up the loose cans and newspapers strewn all around.

She thanked me softly, and then went back into her house without another word.

The next day, a Saturday, I couldn't get my neighbor out of my thoughts. Those boys had only said out loud what I'd been thinking, and I was ashamed of myself for it. I was trying my hand at another batch of Halloween cookies while Darren ripped up the carpeting in the small second bedroom, the one we hoped would someday be a nursery. The wall-to-wall carpeting was badly worn, and when Darren had pulled up a corner, we'd discovered the beautiful hardwood floors underneath.

My new-and-improved cookies turned out better than the first batch had. I frosted them with orange icing and arranged them proudly on a plate, and then I took them into the bedroom to show Darren.

"Hey, these really are good," he said after biting into a warm cookie.

I looked down at the plate. "I think I'll take some over to our neighbor."

"Stephanie? Good idea. Her boys'll love them."

"No, not Stephanie. Our other neighbor—the old lady."

Darren leaned over and gave me an orange-frosting kiss on my cheek. "Babe, I think that would be really nice."

I arranged a few cookies on a small, pretty plate and walked over to the house next door. I knocked on the front door. It took my neighbor so long to answer that I was beginning to think she wasn't home, but finally, she opened the door a crack and peered out.

"Hello," I said, my voice cheerful to cover the nervousness I felt. "I'm your neighbor next door. I just finished baking a batch of cookies and I thought you might like some." I held the plate out as proof of my good intentions.

She stared at me for a long moment, her watery eyes suspicious. Then her expression softened, and she opened the door a little wider. "Thank you, dear," she said in a tiny, wizened voice. "I thought maybe you were those boys again. Sometimes they ring the bell and run."

"I know the mother of one of those boys; I'll let her know about what's going on. She'll put a stop to it—I promise you that."

She smiled, reached a trembling hand out, and carefully took the plate from me.

I learned then that my neighbor's name was Agnes Dimlow, and that she'd lost her husband about a year earlier. After being married for over fifty years, Agnes was having a very hard time taking care of her house and yard by herself. She had one daughter who lived in California, and though her daughter tried to help as much as she could, it was hard for her to do much from so far away.

"I've seen you looking around your backyard a couple of times," I said, bringing up the subject carefully the next time I saw Agnes. I'd stopped at her front door to tell her that I was going to the market, and to ask if she needed anything.

"I lost my wedding ring back there," she told me, her pale lips trembling. "I was pulling up some of the dead weeds around a little flowerbed and my ring flew off. It happened about two months ago, and every time I go back there now, I look for it, but I just can't seem to find it. I'm afraid to even try to mow the lawn. What if I run over it with the mower?"

My heart went out to this old woman who'd never really learned to take care of certain things by herself. My mother had had a difficult adjustment period, too, after my father had passed away, and my mother wasn't nearly as old as this woman was. Agnes came from a different generation than I did; she'd never learned to drive, or to really take care of the necessities of a house and yard. Her husband had done all of those things for her throughout their marriage.

I also thanked God that I had Darren. But, though Darren did a lot of the main repairs and kept my car in running order, I, too, often mowed the lawn myself, and I knew how to tighten a leaky pipe, and, if it were to ever become necessary, I knew I'd be able to take care of myself.

Together, Agnes and I went out to her backyard one morning to look for the lost ring. She showed me the general area where she thought her ring had disappeared, and I got down on my hands and knees and searched through the tall grass.

I found it! It took me almost an hour, but when I held that ring up high for her to see, the expression of joy on Agnes's face made every minute of my "treasure hunt" worthwhile.

A couple of days later, Darren went next door and mowed Agnes's yard, clearing out as much of the brown, late-season grass as he could. He also fixed her back door and a couple of shutters, and ordered a new pane of glass for the cracked window.

I spoke to Stephanie about Benji's teasing. Stephanie called Benji into the room immediately and scolded him, her index finger waving in his face. The boy hung his head and promised he'd pass the word on to his friends that they were not to bother Agnes anymore.

"You won't tease anyone," Stephanie emphasized. "That is something I will not put up with."

Agnes showed me how to make a really excellent beef stew in the Crock-Pot, and I helped her comb her long hair and put it up in a pretty-looking bun. She had trouble doing this herself, because of her arthritic hands. I finally made a gentle suggestion to her about her hair, and she agreed. Then I made a phone call, and the very next day, Kim came over and cut Agnes's hair into a shorter, more manageable style.

"It takes ten years off of you, Agnes," Kim told her when she was done, holding up a hand mirror so Agnes could see for herself.

Touching her hair, Agnes beamed.

On Halloween night, Agnes came over and helped me greet the trick-or-treaters. We passed out candy to the little goblins and superheroes who came to the door, but our biggest laugh of the night came when a group of preteen boys, Stephanie's son, Benji, among them, appeared on the front porch. I put my arm around Agnes's shoulders and we laughed together at the boys' expressions of open-mouthed astonishment.

You see, on that fun-filled Halloween night, I was dressed like a black cat in tights and a sewn-on tail, and Agnes, showing her keen sense of humor, was dressed as . . . a witch!

THE END

117

A GHOST STORY
It Was A Halloween Like No Other

"I don't believe in ghosts," proclaimed Lindsay, taking another draw on her chocolate milkshake.

"Well, I do. And if you had listened to as many ghost tales as I did growing up, so would you," I said, taking another bite of my tuna salad sandwich.

Each day at noon the four of us—Lindsay, Brenda, Alice, and I—get together in the office break room to eat lunch and discuss whatever topic pops up. On that particular Monday, with Halloween only a couple of weeks away, it just so happened to be ghosts.

"I'm with Megan. I think there are spirits that walk this earth."

"Brenda, you always side with Megan. Before I believe in them, I'll have to see one with my own two eyes," Alice declared and went back to her salad.

I swallowed the last bite of my lunch. "My grandmother called them haints and spooks. She told me she once lived in a house where, after she went to bed, she heard footsteps come up the stairs and stop in front of her bedroom door. The door never opened and after a few moments, the footsteps took the same path away until they completely faded."

"That gives me goose bumps." Brenda shivered.

Alice laughed. "Like I said, I'll have to see one."

"How would you like to sit in on a real séance?" Lindsay spoke up, smiling impishly.

I couldn't tell if she was kidding or not. "And how are we supposed to do that?"

"My aunt, Bernadette, is obsessed with ghosts. She and her friend, Louise, belong to some club where they participate in séances. According to Aunt Bernadette, the club has actually contacted spirits. Of course, it's my opinion that someone making the stuff happen, but I don't tell her that. Well, what do you think?"

"I don't know," said Brenda. "Sounds awfully spooky."

"Oh, come on. It'll be fun. Besides, we won't let any old ghost get you," Alice teased.

"Well, okay," Brenda reluctantly agreed. "But if things gets too strange, I'm leaving."

I looked at my watch and stood up, brushing crumbs from my lap. "Count me in. I'd love to have the chance to participate in a séance. Lindsay, when do you think you'll talk to your aunt?"

"We're having dinner together tonight. I'll let you know something tomorrow."

It just so happened that Aunt Bernadette's club had plans to go to a séance that very Friday. They were thrilled that Lindsay and her friends wanted to tag along. We left together right after work, with Lindsay driving and following Aunt Bernadette's directions.

She stopped the car in front of an old, two-story house partially hidden by a cove of ancient oak trees.

"This is the place. Creepy looking, isn't it?"

Brenda frowned. "Too creepy, if you ask me."

We walked along an ivy-draped fence and entered the property through an iron gate that clanged shut behind us, causing us all to jump. On our walk up to the house, I thought I saw a movement from an upstairs window, but when I stopped and looked, there was nothing. I shrugged it off as my overactive imagination and the spooky surroundings.

Aunt Bernadette greeted us at the front door, wearing a black caftan and holding a candle in her hand.

"Lindsay, dear, you don't know how thrilled I am that you and your friends decided to join us tonight. Follow me, girls. You're in for a treat."

The door opened up into a large entryway. Across the room from us, a staircase curved up to a second floor. We turned left into what was once the parlor. A large table sat in the center of the room, surrounded by chairs. Dark draperies covered the windows, blocking any light from the outside. Bunches of candles sat about the room, casting eerie, twisting shadows across the peeling wallpaper. Two middle-aged gentlemen, Tim and Lou, and an older lady, Aunt Bernadette's friend, Louise, were introduced to us, along with three others: Josephine, Delia, and Phyllis.

A woman walked into the room. "It's time for us to get started. Would everyone please take their seat?"

I'll admit I felt a certain excitement as I chose a seat between Alice and Brenda. Lindsay sat across the table from me, flanked by the middle-aged gentlemen, while Aunt Bernadette and Louise sat on either side of the lady who seemed to be in charge.

The woman cleared her throat and the room grew quiet.

"Good evening, everyone. I am Abigail Wheeler, the medium for tonight's séance. Before we begin, I want to tell you a bit about the history of this old house.

"In 1899, Martin Smith commissioned it to be built for his new wife, Lilly Curtis Smith, as a wedding gift. From the beginning they were dubbed a perfect match. After several years, the relationship became strained as it became evident that Lilly would never conceive

119

a child. Martin Smith began staying away from home more and more, and Lilly confided in a close friend that she believed there was a mistress. Poor Lilly became withdrawn and kept to her room.

"Before long the news reached her that her husband's mistress was carrying his child, the one thing she'd been unable to do as his wife. She sank into a deep depression until that fateful morning the housekeeper found her dangling from the end of a rope tied to the banisters at the top of the stairs. We are here tonight to contact Lilly Smith. It is said that her spirit roams this house and has been seen watching intently for her husband's return from her bedroom window."

Even though it was quite warm in the parlor, a chill ran down my spine and I shivered. Could that have been Lilly's window? I believe that spirits walk the earth; I just wasn't sure if I was ready to meet one face-to-face.

Abigail looked around the room. "Extinguish all of the candles, but the one in the middle of the table."

Aunt Bernadette complied and sat back down. Nothing was visible in the room, but the faces of the people around the table.

"Now, everyone hold hands, close your eyes, and clear your minds. A clear mind is a receptive mind."

I did as she said, clearing my mind as much as possible under the circumstances. Brenda was squeezing my right hand so tightly my fingers were beginning to ache.

I leaned close to her and whispered, "You're cutting off my circulation."

"Quiet! I must have absolute quiet!" demanded Abigail.

Once Brenda loosened her death grip on my hand, I concentrated on what the medium was saying. Since it was my first séance, I didn't want to miss a thing. I opened my eyes.

Abigail sat with her eyes closed, her head tilted forward. "Lilly, if you can hear me, give us as sign. We mean you no harm; we just wish to contact you."

The room was quiet, except for the sound of our breathing, deathly quiet.

"Lilly, join us here at this table. We would very much like to contact you."

Suddenly, Abigail slumped over in her chair, as limp as a dishrag. Her chin rested on her chest and her mouth was slightly ajar. She began moaning softly, then louder, and louder. She suddenly sat upright and began speaking in a voice that wasn't her own.

"Martin." She wept. "I loved you."

Her features seemed to shift before my eyes. As the weeping turned to wailing, my heart was pounding like a hammer against my chest and Brenda's hand was trembling in mine. Then Abigail threw her head back and a bloodcurdling scream cut through the darkened room like a knife.

Brenda let go of my hand and darted for the front door like she had the devil at her heels. Lindsay, Alice, and I weren't far behind. I don't know how any of us found the front door in the dark house, but we didn't stop running until we reached the iron gate.

Brenda stood bent over, her hands on her knees, trying to catch her breath. "I've never been so scared in my entire life. I don't know why I let you talk me into things."

"Well, I for one can't remember when I've had that much excitement."

Lindsay pulled her car keys out of her pocket. "Me, either, but I'm ready to go home."

"I'll probably hear that woman screaming in my dreams," declared Brenda, the first one to reach the car.

I looked back at the house. A woman dressed in white stood staring out a window on the second floor, the same one I had observed earlier.

"Who do you suppose that is in the window?" I asked.

Alice laughed. "Maybe it's Lilly."

I shiver and got in the car.

Monday at noon, the four of us gathered around our usual table. I'd gone to visit my parents over the weekend and hadn't spoken to the girls since they dropped me off on Friday night.

"Well, Brenda, did the séance give you nightmares?" I took a sip of my diet Coke.

"Are you kidding? I didn't even turn the lights out in my apartment all Friday night. When that woman became possessed by the spirit of Lilly, I thought I was going to faint."

We all laughed. "You know the whole thing was a show," Alice declared. "I'll bet she was no more possessed by a spirit than I was." She smiled, pulling off the remainder of the crust from her sandwich.

I leaned back in my chair and looked at her over my Coke. "I, for one, believe it was for real. Don't tell me you're still skeptical after what you witnessed?"

Alice shrugged her shoulders. "It's going to take more than an old lady pretending to be someone else and screaming at the top of her lungs to persuade me that spirits hang around after death."

"Megan, I ate lunch with Aunt Bernadette on Saturday and I told her what you said, about seeing someone in the upstairs window. You won't believe what she said." She took another bite of her meatball sub.

"Lindsay, stop eating and tell me," I said anxiously.

She swallowed. "No one had gone upstairs, and nobody else was in the house. Aunt Bernadette said you saw the ghostly figure of Lilly Smith watching out her bedroom window for her husband's return."

Alice rolled her eyes. "Hogwash! It was just your imagination, Megan."

"But, what if it's not hogwash? What if it really was the spirit of that poor lady?" Brenda interceded.

The break room grew quiet as we pondered what Brenda had just said. Then I got an idea. "Why don't we go check the house out on our own? After all, Saturday will be Halloween and since were a bit too old to play dress up, this could be our best Halloween yet."

Brenda looked at me like I'd lost my mind. "You have got to be kidding, Megan. Didn't you get enough of that place on Friday? I sure did."

"Oh, Brenda, you know you're as curious as the rest of us. How about it?"

She didn't answer me immediately. "I'll think about it."

"What about you two?"

"Sure, why not. I've nothing better to do," declared Alice.

Lindsay raised her hand. "Count me in. Anything's got to be more exciting than my love life as of late."

We made plans to meet at the mall and ride together to the Smith house around four o'clock on Saturday afternoon. Though night comes early in October, I wasn't brave enough to go back in that house in the pitch dark, especially on Halloween. I hadn't told the others, but ever since the séance I hadn't been able to get the mysterious lady in the window out of my mind. If it was all a farce I wanted to know, and if it was the real thing, I wanted to know that, too. And that meant checking out that bedroom.

We got a good look at the outside of the house in the daylight. The inside was in better shape than the outside, which needed some paint and several broken windowpanes repaired. As we walked up the brick walk, made uneven by numerous cold winters, I kept my gaze on the upstairs window.

I turned the knob and the door didn't budge. I shoved my shoulder against the door, not very hard, but nonetheless the doorjamb shattered and I practically fell through the door. Lindsay and Alice followed me inside, but Brenda hung back.

"Aren't you coming inside?" I asked.

"I don't know if I want to. I wasn't happy the first time I was here, and I'm not happy now."

"Oh, Brenda. If there are earthbound spirits roaming this house, they haven't harmed anyone."

She cocked her head sideways. "And just how do you know that, Megan?"

Brenda had me there. "Well, have you ever heard of any one being harmed in this house?"

"No."

"See, what did I tell you?"

"Guys, in case you haven't noticed, it's getting darker and darker while the two of you debate," Alice pointed out.

I looked toward the stairs. They looked more foreboding than I remembered. "Okay, let's go. Brenda, you can wait on the porch if you don't want to come along."

She sighed and stepped through the open door. "Alright, I'll go with you," she said reluctantly.

Inside the house, the light grew dimmer by the minute. We took out the flashlights we'd brought along and began to look around.

I wanted to go upstairs to satisfy my own curiosity, so I headed for the curved staircase that wound to the left, ending at the landing where Lilly Smith had hanged herself many years before.

Lindsay was behind me, with Brenda bringing up the rear. The century-old steps creaked beneath our combined weight, sending eerie echoes bouncing off the walls of the empty house. Reaching the landing, we stopped and took a look around.

A cool breeze blew past me. "Did anyone else feel that?"

"If you're talking about the breeze, then yes," said Alice. "Probably came from a broken window."

Lindsay trained her flashlight on the banisters. "Poor woman, she must have felt so sad and depressed to hang herself like that. If I were Lilly, I'd never return to relive that awful memory in this house."

Surprised, I looked at her. "I thought you were a skeptic."

"Well, I am, sort of. It's just that this place makes a person wonder."

"Where do we go from here, Megan?" Alice positioned her flashlight on the floor below.

"Let's take a look in the bedroom where I saw the lady in white. We should be able to tell if anybody's been moving around in there."

I started down the long hallway, pointing the beam of light up ahead. I paused to take a look in the first of the bedrooms and then moved on to the next. "I think this is the one. Come on and help me look for any sign that somebody's been in there."

I walked over to the window and looked out. It was the right bedroom. We were there for a couple of minutes when the air became thick with the scent of perfume.

"Does anyone else smell perfume?" I asked.

Lindsay sniffed the air. "I do, clearly."

"It wasn't here when we came in." Alice didn't offer an explanation, which wasn't like her.

Brenda took hold of my arm and pulled me toward the door. "I think we've been here long enough. First it was that breeze that came from out of nowhere. Now, there's the smell of perfume. Let's get out of this place before something happens."

I pulled my arm out of Brenda's grasp. "Did anyone find anything?"

Lindsay and Alice shook their heads. Brenda grabbed me by the arm again. "Me, either. Now, can we go?"

"Alright, let's go." I sighed. The dust in the bedroom hadn't been disturbed. One thing was certain. No mortal had been standing at that window.

I followed the others back to the landing and took a last look behind me. At the other end of the hall I saw something I couldn't quite make out.

"Look at that. What do you think that is?" I pointed down the hall.

They pointed their lights in the direction of mine. Alice squinted. "Whatever it is, it's getting closer."

The air suddenly became much colder. We stood frozen in place as we watched the apparition come closer and closer, and its identity became apparent. Lilly's spirit did indeed still roam the halls. I couldn't be certain if she was looking at us or through us. She was within a few feet of us when Brenda sprang to life and ran down the stairs, screaming at the top of her lungs. I brought up the rear, the hair on the back of my neck standing up as I expected her to reach out and grab me at any moment. As I raced out the front door, I came face-to-face with a man. Unable to stop, I hit him full force, knocking him off the porch and into the yard. And I landed right on top of him.

I was mortified. "I'm very sorry. I didn't see you," I stammered.

He got up and dusted off his jeans. "Ladies, you're trespassing on private property. I'm Officer Joe Chalmers. Give me one good reason why I shouldn't arrest the bunch of you."

I cleared my throat. "Maybe I can explain. We were here last weekend and we sat in on a séance with some other people. We didn't know we would be trespassing if we came here tonight."

He propped his hands on his hips and looked at me like I had sprouted a horn in the middle of my forehead.

"I don't give much credence to séances and that sort of stuff. All I know is that the caretaker saw lights on the second floor and called the office. I was off duty and I volunteered to check it out on my way home. He thought it might be a bunch of kids messing around, doing Halloween pranks. Wait until I tell him it was a bunch of grown women."

I felt my temperature rise beneath his scrutiny.

124

"But there is one other thing I want to know. What were you running from?"

Brenda spoke up. "The ghost of Lilly Smith."

Joe chuckled and shook his head. "You can't be serious."

"She's right. I wouldn't have believed it if I hadn't seen it with my own eyes," Alice explained.

Lindsay pointed to the house. "Officer, I've always been somewhat of a skeptic, not as much as Alice there, but tonight has made a believer out of me."

He looked at me. "What about you?"

"Me? I've always been a believer, but even I wasn't ready to see Lilly's spirit floating down the hall a foot off the ground toward me. It was quite unnerving."

"How did you get inside? Only the caretaker has the key."

I shoved my hands into the pockets of my jeans. "Well, I pushed on the door. The wood around the lock was sort of rotten." I had to admit, I sounded like a burglar.

He shook his head in disbelief. "I'll need all your names and addresses. I'll let the owner know what happened here. It's up to him whether or not he presses charges." He looked directly at me. "You don't look like the sort of lady who goes around breaking into houses. I hope this one was your first and last."

"It will be," I promised. "Next time I'll use a key."

"That's better. All of you follow me back to my car so I can get your information."

We stopped beside a black SUV and waited while Officer Joe took a notebook off the passenger seat. He flipped to a clean page. "Now, I need names and addresses, beginning with you." He pointed at me.

I sat in the passenger seat while he wrote down my information, using the interior light to see. He was handsome, and I noticed he wasn't wearing a wedding band. For some odd reason that made me feel good.

"I'm really sorry you have to do this on your time off, especially on a Friday night. You probably had a date or Halloween party we're keeping you from."

He looked up at me for a moment. "No date, no party, either." He went back to writing.

Nothing more was said until he finished with me. He handed me my driver's license and smiled. "Okay, you can go. Send in the next one."

When I reached for my license, he held on briefly before turning it loose. I looked up and our gazes locked. The attraction I had for him was nothing like I had ever experienced in all my twenty-six years.

Before I did or said something completely stupid, I got out and sent Brenda his way. I waited in my car for the detective to finish and drove the others back to the mall to pick up their cars.

I went home and took a shower, wondering if the excitement strumming through my veins was due to Lilly's ghost or the handsome detective.

The phone rang, and, deep in thought, I nearly jumped out of my skin. "Hello?"

"Megan Hayes?" A pause on the line.

"Yes, who is this?"

"This is Detective Chalmers. Sorry to call so late. I thought you'd like to know that the caretaker isn't going to press charges, but he does want the door fixed as soon as possible. I assured him that you would personally see that it was taken care of. Was I correct?"

His voice flowed over the phone like syrup over pancakes. "Yes, certainly. I'll call a carpenter first thing in the morning."

"Miss Hayes?"

"Please, call me Megan."

"Megan, I was wondering if you might have dinner with me tomorrow night, that is, if you don't other plans."

I danced in place, silent screams of joy coming out of my open mouth. Max, my cat, thought I had gone insane and dashed under the bed. "Let me think. No, I don't have any plans. I would be happy to have dinner with you."

"Great! I'll pick you up at seven."

"Fine, let me give you my address."

"Never mind, I already have it."

"Oh, yeah, that's right. I'll see you at seven."

I thought seven o'clock would never come. We drove to a little place that was decorated retro Fifties and sat in a private booth across from one another, while Elvis belted out, "You Ain't Nothing But A Hound Dog" on the jukebox.

I took a sip of my sweet tea. "I hope I didn't hurt you last night. I did hit you pretty hard."

"I'll live, but I would like to know something."

"What's that?"

"What really happened in that house?"

"Like I told you last night, we saw a ghost."

I told him the story of Lilly's life. About how she roams the hall of the old house because her spirit can't rest. "I've always believed. Last night was only a confirmation of that belief."

They brought our dinner then, and we spent the rest of the evening talking about our hopes and dreams. And I decided I could easily fall in love with Joe.

Joe drove me home and walked me to the front door. "Megan, I had a great time tonight."

"Me, too."

"I'd like to see you again, soon. After all, it's not every day that I find a girl who knocks me off my feet," he said, and then he kissed me.

THE END